"I got it!"

The little girl pulled [...] and retrieved the cane.

"You're a good helper," Pastor David said as she handed it to him.

"I pick up things for my grampa all the time."

Grampa?

Abe blinked, doing the math. If the judge truly was the child's grandfather, she had to be Rosemary's, since she was an only child. And Abe knew exactly who the father was.

"This is Georgia. My daughter." Rosemary laid her hand on the girl's shoulder and dropped her voice to a whisper. "We need to talk. Later."

The knowledge struck him like an uppercut to the gut. He resisted the urge to sink into the foyer sofa. Instead, he drew a deep breath and took in the little girl's dark curls, quick dimples, denim-blue eyes—Rosemary made over. Only the shape of her mouth was Abe's. Still he couldn't quite take it in.

Her daughter…and his. As sure as the sunrise, he knew it was true.

And Rosemary had kept Georgia a secret from him for four years.

Christina Miller left her nursing job to become a writer and editor so she could read for a living. With two theology degrees, she is a pastor's wife and worship leader. She enjoys exploring museums and hosting Dinner Church in her home. She lives on her family farm with her husband of thirty-two years and Sugar, their talking dog. Contact Christina through Love Inspired, Facebook.com/christinalinstrotmiller or @clmauthor.

Books by Christina Miller

Love Inspired

Finding His Family

Love Inspired Historical

Counterfeit Courtship
An Inconvenient Marriage

Visit the Author Profile page at Harlequin.com.

Finding His Family

Christina Miller

LOVE INSPIRED
INSPIRATIONAL ROMANCE

LOVE INSPIRED®
INSPIRATIONAL ROMANCE

ISBN-13: 978-1-335-55442-0

Finding His Family

Copyright © 2021 by Christina Miller

PLEASE RECYCLE
THIS PRODUCT IS RECYCLABLE

Recycling programs
for this product may
not exist in your area.

This is a work of fiction. Names, characters, places and incidents are either the product of the author's imagination or are used fictitiously. Any resemblance to actual persons, living or dead, businesses, companies, events or locales is entirely coincidental.

This edition published by arrangement with Harlequin Books S.A.

For questions and comments about the quality of this book, please contact us at CustomerService@Harlequin.com.

Love Inspired
22 Adelaide St. West, 40th Floor
Toronto, Ontario M5H 4E3, Canada
www.Harlequin.com

Printed in U.S.A.

Jesus said unto her, I am the resurrection,
and the life: he that believeth in me,
though he were dead, yet shall he live.
—*John* 11:25

In loving memory of my father, James Fill,
who fought back against Parkinson's.

Acknowledgments

I wish we could include the names of
an author's whole team on the spine of a novel.
I could not have written this book without:

Natchezites Ronald and Eleanor Frye,
innkeepers at beautiful Devereaux Shields; and
Caroline Deason, who assisted me with research

The Rock Steady Boxing coaches and volunteers
at Tri-County YMCA in Ferdinand, Indiana

Julie Arduini, Bunny Bassett, Marie Bast,
Kathleen Friesen, Linda Hoover, Heidi Kortman,
Laura Hilton and Linda Maran,
my ACFW Scribes 202 critique group

Susan Holloway, Lisa Jordan and Dana R. Lynn,
my brainstorming partners

Steve Laube, my fabulous agent and wise friend
who always keeps me balanced and encouraged

Dina Davis, my tireless, talented editor and friend
who is a gift from God to me

Linda Fill, my mother, who sits up late to read
and proofread each chapter and cheer me on

Jan, my preacher-husband and watchman on the
wall who is my inspiration for every hero I write

Jesus, my Friend, Savior and soon-coming King;
I long for Your appearing

Chapter One

The problem with a small town was that no one ever forgot your past, and nobody knew that better than Abe.

He shouldered his way inside and through the crowded foyer of Armstrong Gym, muttering apologies and catching a pungent whiff of sweaty towels as he reached to snatch up the half-dozen empty water bottles overflowing the corner trash can. Apparently his new janitor hadn't shown up for work last night—again. The man was making it easy for the town of Natchez to buy into the old reputation.

The one Abe Armstrong was risking everything to reverse.

He smashed the plastic bottles into the can and headed for the front desk, where his barely eighteen-year-old receptionist couldn't seem to look up from her phone. "Mackenzie, what's going on? Did you check into this class?"

Her gaze still on the hot-pink extension of her hand, she pivoted in Abe's direction. "Jase said they should wait here until he cleaned up the boxing room for them."

His brother was back. Good. "Did he find Pastor David?"

Mackenzie finally looked up. At least Abe had found something to take her eyes off that screen of hers. "He still isn't here, and he's never late for class. Jase says he's not answering his phone either."

And he hadn't come to the door five minutes ago when Abe had all but knocked it down. If Pastor David hadn't been so committed to helping with the Rock Steady Boxing class, and if Parkinson's hadn't made him prone to falling, Abe wouldn't have been as concerned...

At the clacking of dress shoes pounding the tile floor behind him, Abe rolled his eyes. Only one person wore Italian wing tips instead of athletic shoes in his gym.

"About time you showed up." Banker JD Turner headed toward him from the boxing room, wearing a black suit that probably cost as much as Abe paid the man in rent every month.

"Of all the times for you to make a surprise visit, this is about the worst," Abe said. "Pastor

David always comes in a half hour before boxing class to help set up, but he's still not here. I just got back from checking on him, so we're running behind."

"Too bad, but you also need to finish fixing up this dump and hire some reliable help if you expect to stay in business," JD said, his voice booming like Abe's had back when he trained his new army recruits.

At least the man hadn't mentioned the smell. Maybe it wasn't as bad as Abe thought.

JD wrinkled his nose. "Start with a decent janitor."

Or maybe it was.

"Because this can't be another charity case." As JD raised his voice, the buzz of chatter in the room suddenly fell silent.

Abe gritted his teeth, determined to keep his own voice low and controlled, despite what this former classmate of his would do. "I've made early payments to you every month since I leased this place. It's not charity, and you know it."

"No, I don't. I know my father felt sorry for your family and gave y'all a place to live after your dad left." JD drew his aviator sunglasses from the top of his head and put them on. "But as for me, this is strictly business. I can't provide for my family and you too."

And just like that, Abe once again felt like the skinny little abandoned boy raised in a shack in a town full of grand old mansions.

Jase caught his attention, heading toward them from the boxing room with fire in his eyes. Abe shook his head, holding up his hand to stop his brother. This was Abe's battle, and no, JD wasn't going to do this to him right in front of the Rock Steady Boxing class. They were here to fight back against Parkinson's, not listen to a bigmouthed banker run him into the ground. "This isn't the time or place to talk business—"

"No, it's time for you to get this gym straightened out," JD called over his shoulder as he started for the entry. "And you'd better keep those payments coming on time."

Before Abe could reply, the man shoved open the door, nearly colliding with a dark-haired woman standing just inside the foyer.

Backing away from JD, the lady snatched Abe's attention. Held it. His breath caught, and for a moment, his heart stopped.

She wore the smile that used to melt him like July ice cream in the sizzling Delta sun, her long pink skirt fluttering as the door closed out the early spring wind. Dark brown curly hair, the sweetest face in Natchez, eyes as clear and blue and bright as the March sky over the Mississippi River.

He turned for a better glimpse of her, and the old rush of emotions hit him hard in the chest, restarting his heart. Yes, after four years, she still looked as beautiful as she had the last time he'd seen her.

Rosemary.

His first and only love. His high school sweetheart.

His wife. But she was now his wife in name only. Except she wasn't even that, since she hadn't changed her name before he left, and he was sure she hadn't done it since.

As his pulse returned to a semblance of normal, so did the pain of the past. Abe rubbed his hands over his eyes. If only she hadn't come home today, when his gym was a mess and JD had run him down in front of everyone. In front of Rosemary.

And then he saw a little girl holding her hand, about the size of his cousin's three-year-old, chattering to the man who had kept Abe and Rosemary apart until their secret wedding. Rosemary's father, Judge Burley Williams, stared Abe down in a silent threat, even though Parkinson's was probably what kept him from scowling at Abe as always.

Rosemary said nothing, clearly waiting for

him to speak first. Which was appropriate, considering how they'd parted. But what do you say to your wife who isn't your wife?

Maybe he should shake her hand. But what man does that? And the way his palms were sweating, no woman would want to touch them. But he had to do something, say something to break the silence, so he slammed his fist onto the foyer table like Humphrey Bogart and did his best Bogie imitation. "Of all the sweat joints in all the towns in all the world, you walk into mine."

As soon as the words were out, he realized how dumb they were. Why remind her of the movie they'd watched during their last evening together? Her favorite movie—the one he'd turned off just before walking out…

"I'm sorry to make things awkward," Rosemary said, her voice still sweet and low as always, but she didn't so much as smile at his twist on the *Casablanca* line.

In the old days, it would have made her laugh. Not today.

"Mama had surgery yesterday, but I couldn't make it here until late last night. So I didn't get a chance to warn you that I'd be coming. Daddy's here for the boxing class. He had his physical therapy assessment last week, so your receptionist told Mama he could start today."

She held him at a distance—her eyes showed it. She hadn't come to see him, that was for sure. This was all about the judge needing boxing classes.

Fine. He could deal with it. He turned to her father. "I'm glad to help you all I can."

"I'm here only because my wife insisted," he said in the quiet voice Abe often heard among the boxers. "Not because I need your help."

No need to worry, Judge. I remember how much you hate me. And how much Abe deserved it, considering his own stupid behavior of the past. The judge would hate him even more now.

The door opened and Pastor David Alston shuffled into the foyer, his quad cane in one hand and his ever-present black Bible in the other. "I hope y'all aren't waiting on me."

Abe looked him over for signs of a fall or some other calamity. "I went to your house to look for you. You okay?"

"Didn't Mackenzie listen to my voice mail? I had to go to the funeral home this morning to help make arrangements for Mark Browning's service." The preacher stumbled, and his cane hit the floor.

"I got it!" The little girl pulled free of Rosemary's hand and retrieved the cane within moments.

"You're a good helper," Pastor David said as she handed it to him.

"I pick up things for my grampa all the time. He says I'm a good helper too."

Grampa?

Abe blinked, doing the math. If she was about the same age as his cousin's girl, and if Rosemary had conceived during the two weeks they were together after their wedding...

If the judge truly was the child's grandfather, she had to be Rosemary's, since she was an only child. And Abe knew exactly who the father was.

He took a step closer to Rosemary. She smelled the same as the last time he'd seen her—a sweet scent she'd called orange blossom. He steeled himself against it. And the child smelled of sunshine and wholesomeness, just as a little girl should.

"This is Georgia. My daughter." Rosemary laid her hand on the girl's shoulder and dropped her voice to a whisper. "We need to talk. Later."

The knowledge struck him like an uppercut to the gut. He resisted the urge to sink into the foyer sofa. Instead, he drew a deep breath and took in the little girl's dark curls, quick dimples, denim-blue eyes—Rosemary made over. Only the shape of her mouth was Abe's. Still he couldn't quite take it in.

Her daughter…and his. As sure as the sunrise, he knew it was true.

And Rosemary had kept Georgia a secret from him for four years.

Abe blew out a breath. "Let's meet in my office after class."

As Georgia sat down on the foyer rug, his cell chimed out his boxing-bell notification. Jase, sending a text. Abe looked around the now quiet, empty foyer. Even Mackenzie had abandoned her desk. At least maybe no one else had heard his dumb Bogart joke.

He pulled out his phone and read that Jase had taken the class to the basketball court for warmups. Abe pocketed the cell again and gestured down the hall. "Class is this way."

Rosemary held out her hand to their child—*their child*—and helped her up.

The foyer grew even quieter, if that were possible.

As he led the way to the boxing room, he sneaked another glimpse of Georgia, his throat tightening at the realization she'd already stolen his heart.

My daughter. At that moment, he vowed to become part of her life, never to let her feel fatherless again. Even though it meant lifelong contact with Rosemary.

He'd find a way. Georgia needed him. Children needed a father who would always be there for them, always protect them, always love them. Not one who never showed up and never provided.

Nobody knew that better than Abe.

Rosemary wasn't sure which was more dangerous—the mix of love and protectiveness in Abe's eyes when he looked at Georgia or the straight-up loathing in Daddy's when he looked at Abe. Or the lingering pain of betrayal she probably revealed through her own eyes when she looked at either of them.

Abe's Humphrey Bogart line had nearly done her in. Of course Abe would try to make her laugh in a difficult moment. Four years ago, it would have made her cry. But those days were gone, because nothing in her life was funny anymore. She'd never watch *Casablanca* again, and she'd already cried all the tears she had over him.

As they veered around the open-concept office area off to the left, Rosemary Williams held tightly to her daughter's hand as if she could hold Georgia back, keep her from getting too close to her father and his untrustworthiness. She couldn't let him break the girl's heart as he had Rosemary's.

She'd always known she'd need to tell him

about Georgia someday, but it wouldn't have been today if Daddy hadn't fallen. Or if Mama hadn't tried to catch him and gone down with him, breaking her arm and wrist.

At least her mother had told Rosemary that Abe started this gym three months ago, right after his impulsive army stint ended and he got home from Afghanistan. But Mama hadn't prepared her for the shock of seeing him again, buff and muscular, all boyishness gone, the shadow of a full beard on his face, his dark blond hair cut in a military fade. Although he wore an Armstrong Gym T-shirt and athletic pants, he looked even better than he had the last time she saw him.

But one thing was sure. If she hoped to keep Abe's contact with Georgia to a minimum, she couldn't swoon over him again. No, she had to remember he'd walked out on her. Abandoning her was one thing, but she refused to let him ditch her daughter.

She caught a glimpse of familiar silvery hair and a trim figure in the weight room off to the right. Sure enough, there stood Grannie Eugenia, using a wipe to disinfect the handles of an elliptical machine before climbing on and starting it up. "What's my grandmother doing in your weight room, Abe?"

"Are you kidding? She was my first member."

Nothing Grannie did totally surprised Rosemary, but she hadn't anticipated this.

As they passed the locker rooms, she wrinkled her nose at the stench wafting out. JD had been right about one thing. Abe needed a new janitor as badly as Rosemary needed to get back to her home on St. Simons Island. Except she couldn't, because you don't run out on your family when they need you.

"Judge, you're going to like Rock Steady Boxing," Abe said, maybe to distract them from the odor. "There's a lot of camaraderie and fun. You probably know some of the people here. They come from all over Adams County and even across the river in Concordia Parish, and they're all friendly."

"Just watch that you don't get too friendly with Rosemary," Daddy said in his Parkinson's-weakened voice. "Or Georgia."

At the almost imperceptible change in Abe's posture, Rosemary picked up on his sense of shame. She still knew her husband well enough to sense his emotions, even from behind. She shoved down an impulse to reach out to him, to assure him he was no longer the fatherless little boy who'd had to accept handouts from his community. She had to guard her heart, not allow herself to be drawn into his fears as before.

She had her daughter to think of now.

Inside the basketball court, his younger brother, Jase, had half the class of about fifteen warming up by batting beach balls at one another. The other half stood in a line doing a team exercise, lifting a long, thick rope over their heads.

From the sound of laughter in the room, Abe had been right—they were having fun. Apparently Jase had shifted his persona from class clown to boxing-class clown. When he saw Daddy and the rest of their little group, he blew the whistle that hung from a cord around his neck, stopping the activity. "We have a new member to welcome."

Abe intercepted a ball rolling his way. "Y'all know Judge Burley Williams and his daughter, Rosemary, who is his corner person." He turned to Rosemary as a murmur started among the class. About Georgia's identity, no doubt. "In boxing, the corner man is the boxer's second. Here, the corner people spot their boxers and help them as needed."

"Who's the little girl, Rosemary? She looks just like you."

No...

Rosemary recognized the elderly woman's voice before she saw her. Eldeen Rogers, her grandmother's friend from the garden club and the biggest gossip in town. Here with her brother, who suffered from Parkinson's, Miss Eldeen was the last person Rosemary would have chosen to hear about Georgia on their first day back in Natchez. But, as Rosemary had decided the day she learned she was pregnant, it was better to let people think she was a single mom than to admit her baby's father—her husband—had abandoned her almost before they'd finished saying "I do."

Georgia ran toward Abe then, reaching for the beach ball in his hands. He opened his mouth and then closed it, glancing at Rosemary with a question hanging in his eyes.

"She's my daughter," she said, watching Georgia take the red-and-white ball from Abe's hands, her little arms stretched around it, barely long enough to hold on.

Rosemary thought back to Grannie Eugenia's phone call two days ago, telling her of Mama's fall. If only her grandmother had told her Abe was home. That way, Georgia could have stayed with Rosemary's boss on the island, raising no questions in their small town and keeping Abe out of the picture…

Then she shook her head. Who was she fooling? She couldn't have left her daughter behind. It would have broken Mama's and Daddy's hearts—and Grannie's.

"The judge needs a boxing name," Jase yelled

over the crowd. "We all have one. How about Brawling Burley?"

Bless Jase for changing the subject. Perhaps he'd sensed the awkwardness. But her father shook his head. Not surprising, since nobody had ever called him by his first name since he became a judge.

"His name is Grampa!" Georgia piped up, dropping the ball and grabbing the older man by the hand.

"All right, then," Abe said. "We'll call him Go the Distance Grampa. Let's do one more warm-up, then we'll put on gloves and head for the boxing room." He positioned her father with the others in a line, gave them basketballs and instructed them to dribble the twenty or so feet to the wall and back.

Amid the distinctive echo of bouncing balls on the wooden floor in the wide, high-ceilinged room, Rosemary's father looked around the court, that expressionless mask settling on his face again. The one that made him look less and less like Daddy every time she saw him.

When her father lost control of the ball and it bounced across the room, Georgia ran after it and brought it back to him. "I got it, Grampa!"

"You can be our helper, Georgia," Abe said, laying his hand on her head and looking like a natural father. "Whenever somebody's ball gets away from them, you can get it and bring it back."

"But you have to walk," Rosemary said. The last thing she wanted was for Georgia to get injured. Or injure one of the boxers. "Be careful not to run into anyone."

Georgia kept busy retrieving balls for the boxers and giving them hugs. Rosemary had to wonder whether some of them turned loose of their ball on purpose, just to interact with her outgoing daughter.

After an hour and a half of spotting Daddy during his balance and footwork exercises and helping him with punching bags and sparring, Rosemary peeled off his red boxing gloves and black liners. The time had come to talk to Abe about Georgia, whether she liked it or not. He'd clearly formed a quick attachment to the girl, but although he was her father, nothing would change. Rosemary and Georgia would soon return to their island home, and Abe was staying here.

Mackenzie showed Daddy and Georgia to the coffee shop next door, the only other business in the former warehouse where Abe had set up his gym. With them gone, Rosemary met Abe in his office for the conversation she'd dreaded.

"Want some water or something else to

drink?" he said, probably unsure how to start this conversation.

She shook her head.

"I don't know what to do about this," he said. "She's my daughter, isn't she?" At her nod, he gestured for her to sit in his mesh desk chair, then took the worn oak one that looked as if it belonged in a musty library somewhere and sat across the desk from her, sipping from an insulated mug. "I never thought I might have a child…"

She knew that voice. He probably didn't realize it, but it was the one he always used when he had to do the impossible but didn't know how. Like when he was twelve and spent all summer mowing lawns and pulling weeds to help with the bills the year his dad left. And when he was fifteen and had to figure out how to fix their secondhand window air conditioner in the July heat.

And when he was twenty and tried to convince Rosemary to tell her parents that they were married…

She shook off the thought. Like Abe, she'd done what she had to do.

"I kept my pregnancy a secret from everyone except my parents. I left town as soon as I discovered I was pregnant."

His face paled, and he seemed a shadow of

himself. "So no one would find out the child was mine."

Yes, but not for the reason he thought. "Nothing will change. We live on St. Simons Island, Georgia, now, and we won't be here long."

"How long?"

"I have two weeks of FMLA leave, which means I have to be back the Tuesday after Easter. Aunt Anjohnette is coming home on Easter to take care of my parents."

"Does your family know I'm Georgia's father?"

She touched her great-grandmother's silver locket, the one she'd never taken off after she'd filled it with Georgia's newborn and one-year pictures. "Only my parents know. I'd like to keep it that way."

"What have you told Georgia about me?"

"Nothing. Every once in a while, she asks where her daddy is. I always tell her it's just me and her."

"And our marriage?"

"Nobody knows except you, me and the justice of the peace."

"Fine." His cheeks began to take on color again, and he stood and paced the floor, which amounted to only about four steps each way. He stopped right next to her and bore through her with those beautiful deep-brown eyes. "Before you leave Natchez, I want Georgia to know I'm her father."

Of course he did. And he'd be his charming, generous self and win their daughter's heart by the end of the day. But once Rosemary and Georgia went home to St. Simons Island, would he move on with his life without them, as he'd done with Rosemary? If so, he'd break their daughter's heart just as he'd broken Rosemary's.

On the other hand, Georgia deserved to know her father. And Abe had a right to hear her call him Daddy.

Nothing about this was going to be easy.

"This is hard for me," she said. "Until I got back to Natchez last night, I didn't know you were here too. I need a little time to think this through."

Judging from his downcast gaze and his tight jaw, he understood her mistrust. That hurt her in a new way.

"What if I want to see Georgia after you're gone?"

Rosemary could hardly deny him an occasional visit, and he couldn't travel to St. Simons Island often, since he had to run the gym. Obviously, he was having a hard time keeping up as it was. "We can talk about that later."

The pacing started again, a habit he must have picked up in the army, since she'd never seen him do it before. "I need to help support her. But honestly, the gym isn't breaking even yet."

No big surprise, judging from what she'd seen—and smelled—today. And what she hadn't seen: a lot of customers. Just two men were working out in the weight room along with Grannie, and she hadn't noticed any other group exercise classes in session this morning either. Clearly the gym was in danger, and if it didn't make it, neither would Rock Steady Boxing.

"You might have figured out that I started the boxing classes for Pastor David. I owe him everything. Without him, it's hard telling what would have happened to Mama, Jase and me after Dad left."

Rosemary had guessed as much. Her gaze traveled the length of the tidy desk until it landed on Abe's Bible and the paperback sitting on top of it. Almost as worn with use as the Bible, the cover had a distinctive 1980s look to it. Sure enough, it was Pastor David's little self-published book, *The Power of the Resurrection*. Older than Rosemary and as worn as Abe's, her copy lay on her nightstand at home.

"The boxing class has slowed the progression of his Parkinson's considerably." Abe picked up the book, ran his finger over its spine and met her gaze. "I can't let this gym go under."

"Mama told me how much better Pastor David is after taking the class for only two weeks," Rosemary said, her stomach knotting a little at the thought of the classes ending. "I want that for Daddy too."

Not to mention that she couldn't go home to the island if he continued to decline, because then, even with Aunt Anjohnette's help, Mama couldn't handle him alone.

"I put the best gym equipment and screens in the weight room and hired our worship leader, Samantha, to build a website. But things aren't falling together like I thought they would. I need more memberships, more traffic through here."

"Part of the problem could be that you've targeted only men," she said. "This place isn't exactly female friendly. I haven't seen any women this morning, other than Grannie and the boxers' corner people. You're missing a whole demographic."

He laid the book on his Bible again. "I'm sure the smell didn't help. Jase's cleaning up the locker room now."

"It's more than that." As sudden inspiration hit her, Rosemary pulled a notepad—her favorite one, with an image of the St. Simons Island lighthouse on the cover—and pen from her purse and started a list. "For one thing, women with small children won't come because they have nowhere to leave them while they work out. You need childcare a couple hours each morning to reach young moms. Do you have an empty room?"

"Are you kidding? This old warehouse is huge. I have a couple of them. What else?"

"Your receptionist needs training. And you need to hire a cleaning crew instead of just one unreliable person." She stopped to think a moment. "You have a whole built-in demographic in the boxing classes—the corner people. Why not give them a discounted membership?"

Abe looked over her shoulder as she made notes about supplies and permits he would need for the childcare area. "How do you know all this?"

"I manage and teach at my church's daycare."

He sat down across from her again, his eyes as intense as on the day he proposed. "How badly do you want your dad to have his boxing classes?"

Rosemary pulled back a little. Had she gone too far, gotten too involved?

"Work with me until Easter. Help me get this gym in shape. Then you can leave and know your dad's taken care of." His expression changed, turning almost unsure, if that could be said about Abe Armstrong. "I want to take a little time to get to know Georgia."

No, no, no...

And let her daughter get attached to him? Working by his side for the next two weeks would be bad enough. No, she couldn't do it.

But if she didn't, this gym would surely fail. And when it did, would her father continue to decline? Would she have to move home and help take care of him and be stuck seeing Abe all the time for the foreseeable future?

Everything she'd read told her this type of exercise was just right for slowing and even reversing some of the effects of Parkinson's.

She knew the answer. She had no choice. Unable to speak, she simply nodded.

But even as she did, she breathed a prayer for God to help her keep an emotional distance from Abe. To keep Abe a safe distance from Georgia.

And to keep everyone's heart intact until she could pack up and take her daughter home.

Chapter Two

With a little grace from God, Abe might pull himself together before Rosemary and Georgia returned to the gym after taking the judge back to work. And he had about fifteen minutes left to do it.

Facing his estranged wife, his unknown daughter and the judge at the same time—disarming Afghani bombs had been easier. Less stressful. Or so it seemed this morning. And yet...

An image of Georgia's cute little face flitted through his mind. He had a daughter. She needed a provider, a protector.

A father.

He let this truth sink in, even as he tried to convince himself to guard his heart. In two weeks, Rosemary would take Georgia hundreds of miles away to their island home. He was staying here. He had no chance of avoiding a painful separation from either of them. They were family, even though he didn't deserve them.

Rosemary leaving him—that was a switch.

Shoving away the thought, Abe grabbed an armload of dirty towels. He packed them into the washer in the gym's mechanical room under his apartment, added soap and turned it on. He had to get his mind—his fears—under control and focus on his job. Because, as of today, he had to help raise and support Georgia. And the gym wasn't even supporting him, let alone a little blue-eyed girl.

To change that, he'd have to keep his heart in check.

He stopped and bowed his head, shot up a silent prayer for God to send that grace—quickly.

Five minutes later, he headed for the space the former tenant had used as a showroom. Opening off the foyer, the high-ceilinged, glass-walled room looked larger than the childcare area at church, even with its piles of empty boxes and mismatched, scratched-up tables and chairs. Rosemary could use the cabinets and countertops on the east wall for her supplies and toys, and there was even a little office off the north wall for her to use. Maybe this would work.

At the whooshing sound of the front door, he turned toward the lobby. Rosemary and Georgia burst in, holding hands and giggling and looking like the happiest little family in Natchez. And when his daughter saw him hovering in the entry to the new childcare room, she broke free of her mother and ran to him, despite not knowing he was her father.

Maintain a distance from Georgia? The chances suddenly plummeted to subzero.

Rosemary spotted him instantly, her smile dying in her eyes.

So did the shred of hope that must have crept into his heart when he wasn't looking.

Abe tamped down the feeling. He'd have to be a lot more careful if he hoped to make it through the next two weeks. Had to focus on the fact that Rosemary had been too ashamed of him to tell her father of their elopement four years ago—and she still was.

A memory rolled through his mind like a Bogart film.

Tell your parents we're married, move out of their house and live with me in my apartment. Prove to me you're not ashamed of me.

No, I need more time...

He'd walked out and joined the army like the fool he was.

A tug on his sleeve pulled him out of his thoughts. He looked down to see blue eyes gazing up at him.

"Mr. Abe, Mama said I can help her make a playroom. I get to help pick the colors." Georgia took his hand as if she'd done so every day of her life.

The smallness of that hand inside his—it ignited a rush of emotion he'd never before felt. Tiny, fragile, depending on him even though she didn't know it, his daughter looked up at him with those impossibly blue eyes that spoke only of trust, gentleness.

Sweetness.

Just like Rosemary's.

The two must have gone home and changed clothes, because instead of her pink skirt and white fluttery shirt, Rosemary now wore jeans and a light blue Faith Island Daycare T-shirt, and in a matching shirt and blue leggings, Georgia looked even more like her mother than before.

He forced himself out the showroom door and trudged with Georgia toward Rosemary. How was this ever going to work?

"You got your dad to his office on time?" Not the smartest thing he could have said, since Rosemary was always early. And he shouldn't have brought up the judge, because her eyes quickly turned guarded.

He knew that look. The judge had said something about him to her, and it hadn't been a compliment.

Seeing it set Abe's heart on the right track again. He was smarter now than he was the first time he'd kissed the daughter of the most powerful man in Natchez.

"His intern, Olivia, had everything ready for him, from her research on a case he's trying right down to the correct flavor of coffee for his pod machine." Rosemary averted her gaze. Avoiding any personal discussion of her father, as always.

Fine. He could sidestep conflict as well as she could. With Georgia now silly-dancing her way across the lobby, he gestured toward the glass-walled room. "Check out this area. I think it'll work for childcare."

"You need an Olivia for your gym." Rosemary lowered her voice, glancing at Mackenzie as they passed the reception desk. As usual, the girl sat staring at her phone screen as if she were in some altered state of consciousness. "Someone who can anticipate the gym's needs—and yours—and can take the initiative to meet them. Someone who's willing to work hard to make your business succeed."

Abe opened the heavy door and held it for them. "I know, but she was Pastor David and Miss Pauline's foster child. She graduated last year, and I gave her this job a couple months before Miss Pauline passed away so she could move out on her own. They loved having her there, but with his Parkinson's…"

Rosemary's eyes softened as she glanced through the window wall at Mackenzie. "Another reason you have to keep the gym open."

"Right."

"I'll work with her. And we need to find a janitor and a few childcare workers and exercise class teachers. I can take care of that if you want."

"Great. And I'll focus on getting this room ready."

When she had Georgia settled on the floor with her coloring books and crayons, Rosemary plopped her backpack onto the counter and drew out a pen and her lighthouse notebook. After opening it to the first blank page, she wrote "Armstrong Kids" at the top of the page and underlined it with a flourish.

"Armstrong Kids?"

Rosemary looked up at him, the sunlight streaming in the east window and turning her eyes to indigo. "At my daycare, we call our students Faith Island Kids, named after Faith Island Church. Armstrong Kids has a great ring to it. You could paint it above the door with a slogan like 'Building strength and character into our smallest athletes.'"

As usual, this woman was miles ahead of him in her thinking. "We're going to turn three-year-olds into athletes?"

She smiled, brushing at a wisp of dark hair that had fallen from her ponytail. "In a manner of speaking. You can buy little dumbbells and weight benches for kids as young as three. They're specially designed to prevent injury. The kids mostly just play with them, but they introduce the children to fitness early in their lives."

It seemed there was a lot Abe didn't know about his own business.

"Well, that's the strength part, but what about teaching character?"

"At Faith Island Kids, we use books and posters to teach them concepts like kindness, respect and hard work. Armstrong Kids can be much more than just a babysitting room. It's an opportunity to impact children's lives."

And this whole overhaul-the-gym thing might turn out to be much more than he'd thought…

"We'll need to build a restroom, maybe in the corner, and get some regular toys too. A refrigerator and microwave." Rosemary glanced at the outside door across the room, then headed that way. "I don't know what our budget is, but a fenced-in outdoor playground would be great."

He gave her the number he'd come up with: a third of his inheritance from his father.

"Abe, you're kidding me. How'd he get that kind of money?" Rosemary said, her eyes wide. "I remember him leaving huge debts behind when he abandoned your family and your mama working hard to pay them, and now you say he left you quite comfortable."

"Yeah, it's too bad he wasn't man enough to pay those debts. But a few years after he moved back to Nashville, where Jase and I were born, he stopped trying to become a recording artist like before and started writing songs instead. He wrote several big hits, and Jase and I still get royalty checks. He never married the woman he left with, so we got it all."

"I admit I never expected that," she said.

Since he'd already spent his savings on gym equipment, renovations and supplies, he didn't want to touch the rest of his inheritance if he could avoid it. Not after living in poverty as he, Jase and Mama had years ago, never knowing if the lights would be cut off or they'd have money for proper meals.

Within an hour, Rosemary had supply lists and to-do lists made for both of them. Surprisingly, he'd begun to reach a comfort level with her. But hadn't she always made him feel at ease, almost confident, as if he were a better man than he was?

Until she hadn't.

He still didn't know how this was going to work, but God had answered his prayer and sent that grace, all right. And apparently, He had sent it through the last person Abe had expected— Rosemary.

Sometimes, when Rosemary looked at her parents, she was surprised God hadn't included the words *opposites attract* in the Bible. Because she couldn't think of many phrases that held more truth.

Her father sat at his great-grandfather's writing desk, his back to them. Mama relaxed in her new leather recliner across the sitting room. Rosemary lay on the antique rug with Georgia, making snap-bead jewelry while supper simmered on the stove, its spicy aroma filling the room.

"I don't like how that boy looks at you," Daddy said in his soft voice that hardly resembled his previously powerful timbre. He lifted his head from his ledger, where he presumably entered the events of his day as always.

Here we go. Rosemary held her tongue. No need to defend Abe when Mama was around.

"He's a grown man, Burley." The fall that brought on the new weakness in Mama's limbs sure hadn't done the same to her voice. She still spoke her mind in the clear, confident tones of the old-school Natchez debutante she'd once been. "Let the past be the past. He's going to help you."

"Abe Armstrong couldn't help a little old lady across the street, let alone do anything for me." Daddy turned halfway in the chair as if to look at them but didn't quite make it. Instead, he faced the corner of the room, seemingly unable to twist in the chair that had sat in the same spot in front of the same desk for two hundred years. "Besides, I don't need help. I'm just stiff."

So Mama had been right. Daddy was still in denial over his diagnosis.

"I meant what I told you this afternoon. I don't want anything developing between you two."

Rosemary glanced at her daughter. It seemed a bit late for that advice. Not that she hadn't heard it every day since Daddy found out about her secret dates with Abe that spring.

If only her father hadn't walked in on their first kiss, in the river bluff gazebo on a starry spring evening after following them from the spring festival while they were still in high school.

She remembered the fire in Daddy's eyes as he looked at her the way he must look at hardened criminals in his courtroom. And she'd never forget her father's words as he drove her home.

Mark my words. If you keep seeing Abe Armstrong, I'll come after him and his family. His mama is about to become a nurse practitioner, and our hospital's HR director owes me a big favor. I can make one phone call and stop her from ever working as a nurse practitioner in Natchez. You know I can do it.

He sure could. Rosemary had seen that side of him many times. And she'd overheard him boasting about letters of recommendation he'd written and references he'd given for local families, and then call in those favors later to take down a perceived enemy. In fact, the more she thought about it, he seemed almost to have a side hustle of revenge going on.

The worst one had been Cody Lewis, the classmate she'd had a crush on back in eighth grade—the one Daddy had caught her kissing at her thirteenth birthday party. As far as Rosemary knew, Cody and his family still lived in Memphis, where his dad got transferred after Rosemary's father had called in a favor with the man's boss.

And he still held the same old grudge as before.

Nobody in the Armstrong family would have been safe if she had revealed their marriage, and Rosemary couldn't be sure that wasn't still the case.

Yet everything might have been different today if that night with Abe at the gazebo had gone another way.

Or not.

At any rate, Daddy clearly had no more use for Abe now than he had then, but Rosemary had never understood why. Sure, Abe's father was a deadbeat dad who'd abandoned his family and taken off with another woman. But when Daddy always said an Armstrong wasn't good enough for his only daughter, did he mean because Abe's father left them? Or because as a failed Nashville musician, Vernon Armstrong had come home to Natchez back when Abe and Jase were toddlers and worked on a factory assembly line, as Cody's dad had?

Regardless, as her father had said in the car this afternoon, he intended that nothing "like that" happened again between her and Abe.

Rosemary was a little surprised he'd said it now, within Mama's hearing.

Her father rubbed his fingertips over the edge of the desk as if smoothing it. "I don't like that boxing class."

Mama cleared her throat—always a sure sign

that she meant to be heard. She held up the arm with a surgical rod attached to it. "I need you to go, Burley. We can't afford another fall. Besides, Abe's a veteran, a business owner and the son of a Natchez native, so stop slamming him. He's done well."

"Cozette, I've never understood why you think an Armstrong is a good match for Rosemary. He'll never be able to provide for her as I have."

As Rosemary had heard a hundred times since that night in the gazebo.

Daddy turned back to his ledger. "What's that smell?"

"Rosemary made something new. Taco soup," Mama said.

"Soup?" Daddy's voice rose louder than Rosemary had heard it in a year. "This is Tuesday. Tuesday is pot roast night."

"Tuesday is taco soup night at our house, Grampa. Mama says you get what you get and you don't throw a fit." Georgia sprang up from the floor and hopped over to her grandfather, carrying a red, blue and green plastic bracelet she'd made. She dangled the gift in front of his face. "Hold out your hand."

Daddy turned his head, looked at her for a moment, then held out his hand. He even let Georgia slide the bracelet onto his wrist.

Thank You, Jesus, that Daddy doesn't reject Georgia as he did me.

The next morning, after helping her mother with her shower and dressing, Rosemary made grits and biscuits and gravy for their breakfast. As raindrops splashed against the kitchen window, she followed Grandma Williams's biscuit recipe and cooked the grits in cream in Mama's double boiler, like a good Natchez girl, hoping it would make Daddy forgive her for taco soup. And maybe the old-fashioned biscuit goodness would soften the blow when she told him of her plans for today.

As she dropped hot biscuits into Mama's cloth-lined bread basket, the east-wing door opened, its hinges creaking their tune in a perfect octave. Within moments, Grannie Eugenia breezed in from her wing, wearing black leggings and a fuchsia athletic shirt and carrying her phone, wireless earbuds and water tumbler. Georgia skipped along beside her, chattering about her grandfather and how he didn't want to go to the gym.

"It's pouring outside. I can't walk or take my golf cart to the gym this morning, so I'll need a ride." Grannie pulled her blender from the cabinet, plugged it in and opened the refrigerator. Then she added blueberries, strawberries, spinach and jars of who-knew-what kinds of supplement powders, along with almond milk, into the blender jar. "Georgia said she met a man named Abe there."

Her blue eyes held a gleam, as if she knew Rosemary's history with Abe. But Daddy had seen to it that Grannie had no idea that Abe was Georgia's father.

Her grandmother turned on the blender and shouted over the noise. "He isn't that handsome Abe Armstrong, is he? Your old beau?"

Beau. Grannie's old-fashioned word caught in Rosemary's heart. It was the word the elderly justice of the peace had used the night she'd stood before him in the shadowy room he'd called his parlor.

Take your beau's hand, young lady...

She had to close her eyes for a moment as the memory of that night rolled over her. She'd thought their love had been strong enough to prove her father wrong. But he'd been right. The years of raising Georgia on her own had attested to that.

Leave it to Grannie to stir up the old memory.

"If you still like him, let me know. I can help." Grannie punched the off button, and the grating sound of the blender faded away. Unlike her grandmother's voice.

"There's nothing you can do to help me, Grannie."

"Remember when Fannie Swan took a trip to New Orleans and came back married?"

"Of course not. Mama hadn't been born yet when that happened." But Rosemary had grown up hearing the story about the sudden, successful marriage of their nearest neighbor.

"I might have helped that relationship along." The older woman leaned in closer, finally lowered her voice. "And they weren't the only ones. I have never failed to bring couples to the altar, once I see the match is good."

What? Rosemary sucked in her breath. Grannie Eugenia was the famed mysterious matchmaker? The one all of Natchez had speculated about for the past sixty years?

"No one knows—"

The sound of footsteps in the dining room cut her off.

Grannie's head swiveled toward the sound, her eyes wide. Then she laid her finger on her lips, gave Rosemary a conspiratorial wink and poured her smoothie into a glass. "Did I guess right? Is Abe Armstrong the man Georgia can't stop talking about?"

Rosemary chanced a glance at her parents, who approached through the dining room. Had Daddy heard Grannie talking about Abe? *Please, God, no...*

"Miss Eugenia," her father said, easing himself into a kitchen chair, "we don't say that name in this house."

What? Since when?

"You bring up his name all the time, Burley." Grannie propped one hand on her slender hip, glaring at her son-in-law. "And you say it in the same tone you always used when you spoke of Abe's father."

"Maybe I did in the past, but not anymore."

"But I like Mr. Abe," Georgia said, a hint of a whine to her voice, as a clap of thunder shook the house.

Rosemary should have anticipated this. She quick-stepped to set the biscuits, gravy, grits and muscadine jelly on the table, then she pulled out her mother's chair and sat Georgia in her booster seat. "Everybody sit down so we can pray."

"I know what you're doing, daughter." Daddy's tone had turned dark as the stormy sky. "You want me to put a biscuit in my mouth so I won't talk about that Armstrong boy."

Grannie stood next to Georgia and spooned grits into the girl's bowl. "Not a bad idea."

No, it would take more than biscuits to do that.

"Y'all bow your heads." Daddy glared at everyone at the table before mumbling his way through a seemingly half-hearted prayer.

According to her plan, Rosemary waited until he'd taken his first bite of biscuit, and then she breathed a quick prayer of her own. "I told Abe I'd help him at the gym this morning. We're going to try to make his business more profitable."

Her father gave her that blank Parkinson's stare that made him look as if he didn't care. But when he got up and pitched the rest of his biscuits and his bowl of grits into the trash can, she knew he did, indeed, care. "I want pot roast next Tuesday."

The front doorbell interrupted his protest.

A visitor before breakfast? Rosemary got up and headed toward the entry hall, peered through one of its lead-glass sidelights.

Abe stood on the front gallery, his clothing and hair soaked with rain.

Not letting herself think about the times he'd stood there in the past, looking around and behind him in case her father lurked somewhere nearby, she opened the door.

"Can I drive you to the gym?" Those brown eyes softened for an instant as he looked at her, but then he cleared his throat and shoved his hands into his pants pockets, his mood seeming to shift. "I thought maybe you could use some help, since it's raining and you've got Georgia to take care of…"

He dropped his gaze to the gallery floor as if he'd just realized how silly his words sounded. As if it never rained on St. Simons Island, and she never had to take Georgia out in it by herself.

She couldn't place the emotion she saw in his face, but it sure wasn't a feel-good one. A mix of uncertainty and the old shame he always carried, maybe. It wasn't quite the same as the look he used to wear when he felt less than the other kids, when he didn't have a proper winter coat or shoes, but something about it triggered her memories of his poverty. And it touched her in an odd way. A way that made it impossible for her to refuse his help.

"I'll get Georgia. She can bring her breakfast along and heat it at the gym. Grannie wants a ride too."

"I'll wait here."

As always, since her father had never allowed Abe inside their home.

For the hundredth time, she saw the discrepancies between their lives, how they'd grown up in two different worlds. Her abundance and his lack. Her estate and Abe's donated shanty. His kind and gentle mother and her father who'd sabotaged any chance she might have had with Abe.

Yes, opposites did attract.

In the past. Not now.

Because as far as Rosemary and Abe were concerned, opposites attracted trouble.

Chapter Three

It seemed as if each drop of cold spring rain had decided to pelt down on Abe's bare head just to remind him that he had no idea how to be a father to Georgia.

For starters, how do you keep a little girl from getting wet and catching cold when you also have a laptop and backpack to carry?

He'd parked his black pickup in front of the gym door and escorted Miss Eugenia inside, so now he ran for Rosemary and Georgia. But Rosemary had already taken their daughter out of her car seat and carried her to the entry, along with the backpack and laptop Abe had intended to bring in, so he merely held the door.

He should have known she wouldn't need his help.

Inside, as Rosemary took off Georgia's raincoat and boots, Abe turned on lights and unlocked the door to the new Armstrong Kids room. "I picked up carpet samples this morning," he said over his shoulder.

"And I selected appliances and toys online last night."

Georgia sat on the floor and snatched a stuffed elephant and penguin from the backpack as Rosemary retrieved her laptop from her messenger bag and powered up. "If we buy the refrigerator, microwave, and office equipment and supplies locally, we'll pay a little more, but we'll also gain a couple of days in delivery time. We need to get done and get back to our normal lives."

Right. But Abe wasn't so sure he wanted his daughter to leave anytime soon…

He glanced over at the girl as she pretended to make the two animals play together. He'd already lost three years of her life. How much more would he miss? "Last night I told my mom about Georgia." He lowered his voice so the little girl couldn't hear him over her own playful chatter. "She invited you, me and Georgia to her house for supper tonight. Crawfish étouffée."

Rosemary's face paled a bit. "Did you tell her we're…"

"Married?" The old sense of betrayal rose up in him before he could stop it. "Of course not. Since you wouldn't let me tell anyone after the wedding, I figured you don't want them to know now."

"Good." Her color returned to normal, but her voice wavered a little.

Proving she was still ashamed of him, as much as before. Even more, because now she'd rather let the whole town think she'd had a child out of wedlock than to name him as Georgia's father.

And that was fine with him. You can't undo the past. He'd found that out long ago. "I wish you had let me know about Georgia. I could have helped. Could have gotten to know her."

"It's no use, Abe." She dropped her voice. "I couldn't involve you with her then, and I can't now. Or ever."

"That's not going to work for me. I want to be in her life, to help raise her. Be a father to her." He leaned against the counter, crossing his arms in front of him. "She's my child, too, Rosemary."

She sighed, the sound of it crushing his hope of a future with Georgia. "There's more to it than that. But yes, we'll come to your mother's house this evening. I always liked her, and she deserves to meet her granddaughter."

What more could there be to it? Georgia was his daughter, and he deserved…

Abe stopped the thought cold. This wasn't

about his rights, and arguing wasn't the answer. He dropped his arms, trying to look less defensive. As a bullheaded twenty-year-old, he'd seen where his ultimatums had gotten him with Rosemary. Better let this slide for now.

But not forever.

An hour later, after they'd chosen and ordered their supplies, Miss Eugenia popped her head into the room. "Would you like me to take Georgia next door to Natchez Coffee Shop for something to drink? I have business over there."

Business?

Rosemary's head shot up from the laptop screen, her mouth open for a moment. "You don't mean…"

Miss Eugenia's eyes twinkled as if she'd discovered the juiciest secret in Natchez. But Abe had given up trying to figure her out a long time ago.

"Grannie, why are you really going over there?" Rosemary said.

"I'm just doing my duty." Grannie took Georgia's hand and headed for the door as if on a mission of some kind. "The coffee shop is a start-up, but it's not doing so well. No wonder, if he can't come up with a more imaginative name than Natchez Coffee Shop. Rance Bailey rented that space in the old warehouse just before Abe took this one. Rance doesn't have an ounce of business sense, just like his grandfather."

A little frown crossed Rosemary's face for an instant. "Is Rance married?"

"Not yet," Miss Eugenia said in a singsong voice.

In the silence that followed their exit, Abe pondered Rosemary's random question. He knew better than to think she'd be interested in the middle-aged man.

Rosemary sighed and pulled up a document. She turned the screen toward Abe. "This is the gym's new marketing plan."

Moving in closer to read, he scanned the headings. Three new social media platforms, a new video channel and—radio? He broke out in a sweat as if he'd just run a triathlon. "I'm not talking on the radio."

"You have to reach all your demographics. Who listens to the local Natchez radio station?"

He didn't care that he was scowling like the judge. "Your grandma."

"Right. And all her friends. Who did you say was your first gym member?"

"Again, your grandma. But that doesn't mean other seniors will come here."

"You might be surprised. I admit Grannie Eugenia is sprier than most ladies her age. But if you start some senior-focused classes, they'll come. And a lot of them babysit their grandkids, so the childcare can pull them in too."

"But what am I going to talk about on the radio?"

She scrolled down the page. "We're going to start a radio and social media blast with tidbits about Parkinson's, Rock Steady Boxing and working out. You can do this. You were great in speech class in school. Besides, you were in the army."

He scanned her list of Parkinson's and RSB facts. It all looked good. "What's the army got to do with it?"

"I heard you used to train new recruits. That means you had to talk to them."

"Not the same."

She blew out a breath. "Now you're a personal trainer instead of an army trainer. Just think of the person you want to reach and talk as if you're speaking with that person."

No way would that work. But Abe couldn't deny that she was a business and marketing powerhouse.

"I've never seen this creative side of you before." Maybe getting away from the judge for a couple of years had helped her find it.

Or maybe it was because she'd been away from Abe…

Or not, because her eyes took on a gleam he recognized but couldn't quite place.

"My job as daycare teacher takes more creativity than law school did. Or at least a different kind of creativity."

That was it. The look in her eyes was the same look she used to get whenever she talked about wanting to become a first-grade teacher. Or about kids or the primary Sunday school class she taught. "You're following your dream now instead of your father's dream for you to become a lawyer."

"In a sense. I still wish I could teach primary grades, but I'm thankful for my daycare job—and that I could finally leave law school."

The glow faded, and she looked away, her mouth a little tight.

Then it hit him. She was thinking of Abe's promise, the one he'd made on their wedding day: if the judge refused to continue to pay for her college after he found out they were married, Abe would work hard and put her through school.

But instead he'd left. Broken the promise. Broken his vows. Because, although he'd never even looked at another woman, he hadn't kept his vows to love and cherish Rosemary.

And hadn't helped to provide for her and Georgia either. What did a church daycare manager make anyway? Could she afford to take online classes to continue her education? For all he knew, she could have half her credits already—or none. Suddenly he had to know. "Are you taking any classes, working toward your dream?"

An emotion—regret or possibly shame—flashed across her face and revealed her answer. "I'm busy with work and taking care of Georgia all week. On Saturdays, I tutor primary-age children, and that money goes into Georgia's college fund."

Yep, just as he'd suspected, Rosemary had been the one to pay for Abe's pride and foolishness. His stubbornness.

Even though he could never fix their marriage, he could fix the situation. Helping Rosemary and providing for Georgia were just two more reasons his gym had to succeed. He'd killed her dream, so he had to revive it. Refresh it.

Resurrect it.

The pouring rain slowed to a drizzle the moment Abe, Rosemary and Georgia pulled up in front of Anise Armstrong's Orleans Street home.

Rosemary pulled her phone from her purse and touched her mirror-app icon. When she saw her image, she wished she hadn't. She resisted the urge to smooth her rain-frizzed hair, since messing with it would only make it worse.

"Your mama bought the Bishop's House?" she said as she closed the offensive app and slid the phone into its little pocket in her purse. "I almost didn't recognize it."

Abe nodded. "It was high time she got out of that shack the banker gave us. It wasn't fit to live in. Especially in proud old Natchez, where there's a two-hundred-year-old mansion or National Register home on every corner."

"Was this house in good shape when she bought it?"

"For a house built centuries ago, yeah. But it needed a landscape renovation. It took her, Jase and me a month of evenings and Saturdays to get it done."

"It looks great. I'm glad you kept those beautiful old crepe myrtles." Rosemary stepped out of the truck and settled her black cross-body bag over her blue cardigan. A week ago, she'd never have dreamed Abe would bring her and Georgia to his mother's house tonight.

She'd always wanted Georgia to know her other grandma—the one who'd lived down the shame of her former husband's abandonment and had eventually lifted her family from the poverty he'd left them in. And who'd also made a name for herself in this town, both as nurse practitioner at the local hospital and as a volunteer at the Historic Natchez Foundation.

And from the looks of this house, Miss Anise was doing quite well.

Abe had sprinted around to the passenger side and opened the back door, so Rosemary reached for her daughter, lifted her from her car seat and wrapped a throw blanket around her. He looked beyond handsome tonight, freshly shaved and wearing jeans and a brown Henley just snug enough to draw the eye to his sculpted shoulders.

"I'm gonna see Mr. Abe's mama," Georgia piped up, her voice shrill with excitement.

More like the grandma she'd never yet met.

Suddenly the whole situation looked a little different. As kind and gentle as Abe's mother was, she'd have been a good grandma to Georgia these past years. A pang of regret threatened to soften Rosemary's resolve to keep Abe and his family in the background of Georgia's life.

But she'd had no choice. Not with his history of running.

And for the Armstrongs' sake, she had to make sure all of them knew this would be a temporary relationship as long as Daddy was alive.

Forcing a smile, she handed off her daughter

to Abe. "Your mama will love seeing Georgia in your arms."

He held her as if he'd done it every day since she was born. "Let's lose this blanket. She's already bundled up."

And let her catch a cold or worse? "No, let's leave it on."

He shrugged and left the throw on.

Inside, the warm air smelled of étouffée and freshly baked bread. A peek into the dining room showed a table set with delicate-looking floral china and an antique cut-crystal vase of fresh purple wisteria.

Miss Anise was still as organized as ever.

Seeing them enter, Abe's mother stuck a bookmark in her paperback romance novel and set the book on the walnut table beside her sofa. Youthful, slim and pretty in her white T-shirt, long pink ruana and destructed jeans, she still wore her blond hair in her signature messy-bun style. She'd been boho long before boho was cool, and she still was.

Taking in the sight of her only grandchild, she slowly rose and took a hesitant step forward, as if the tears glistening in her eyes had blurred her vision.

To be honest, Rosemary's vision seemed a bit hazy too.

"Georgia," the older lady said, her voice wavering.

When Georgia leaned toward her grandmother, arms outstretched, Rosemary had to look away. Why did it have to be like this?

Of course, she knew why. Because her father always followed through on his threats. If he ever suspected Rosemary had feelings for Abe again, he'd do what he'd promised: ruin the Armstrong family.

And he could do it. He'd done it before. She remembered his threat of this evening.

Just so you know, I never did call in that favor with the HR director at the hospital. Nothing has changed, Rosemary. I could still have Anise Armstrong let go from her job.

Why couldn't he just leave Abe's family alone?

"Rosemary, she's a beautiful, happy girl. You're doing a good job with her," Miss Anise said over Georgia's chattering as she held the girl. Still as gracious as always.

Then Rosemary realized Abe hadn't said a word since they got there. She glanced at him pacing across the room, his face hard as the marble fireplace mantel. Rosemary went to him, afraid of what that expression might mean.

"That look on Mama's face—" he whispered,

then he swallowed hard. "It's going to kill her when you take Georgia away."

"Take her home. Not away."

"However you say it, everybody's going to get hurt…"

His voice trailed off, and she whispered a prayer that he would understand, would make peace with this bad situation. If only she could tell him the real reason she had to take Georgia back to the island, he'd understand.

But he still wouldn't agree.

Five minutes later, around the table, Abe's prayer clearly came from the heart. A big change from the rote prayer he'd always said back in the day. By the time they all said "Amen," Rosemary felt as comfortable in this inviting home as she did in her own house. Or her parents'.

Come to think of it, she'd been just as much at ease in the run-down bungalow Abe had grown up in.

"How did you keep Georgia a secret this long?" Miss Anise said as she passed the crawfish-vegetable-hot-sauce dish. "I'm sure nobody in Natchez knows about her."

"For one thing, I closed my social media accounts, and I'm not in contact with my old friends. My parents visit every few months, so we don't need to come here. I haven't been home since she was born."

"I don't understand why you kept her a secret from Abe and me," Miss Anise said, her gaze fixed on her only grandchild.

If Rosemary had heard even a trace of bitterness or judgment in the older woman' voice, she could have continued to justify her actions. Now she hesitated.

At nineteen, pregnant and alone, she'd had no choice but to do as Daddy said: leave town and tell no one that she was carrying Abe's child. Now maybe it was time to decide for herself, to let Miss Anise have the joy of being a real grandmother, showing Georgia's pictures to her friends and bragging about the little girl's milestones.

Except Daddy would find out and carry out his threat.

She closed her eyes as an image of her junior-high crush, Cody Lewis, flashed through her mind, waving goodbye from the back seat of his father's beat-up van. Daddy sure hadn't lost any time getting Cody's factory-worker father relocated to a plant in Memphis after he'd caught him kissing Rosemary on that long-ago day. Her father could do the same now—this time with Abe and Miss Anise. Maybe even Jase.

How had everything gotten so complicated? And when had her father become such a bully?

Owing Abe's mama an explanation, she

spooned a small serving of étouffée onto Georgia's plate and passed the dish. "You know Daddy. He demanded we keep Georgia's father's identity a secret, and he always gets his way."

Hopefully, that would satisfy them both.

"I'm surprised the judge let you bring Georgia to Natchez," Abe said.

"Mama shamed him into it. She said that if he'd joined Rock Steady Boxing back when Pastor David did, Daddy's balance might be improved now, too, and they might not have both ended up on the floor. When she put it that way, my father agreed to let her come. Besides, he dotes on Georgia and wanted to see her."

In the awkward silence, Rosemary tasted the étouffée. Wow, it was as good as she remembered. And it was time for a change of subject. "Your home is beautiful. How long have you lived here?"

"I bought this house when I finished grad school. I furnished it little by little." Miss Anise touched one of the wisteria sprigs cascading over the crystal vase in the table's center. "And this vase was my graduation gift to myself. When I started college, I made a promise to buy a decent home and one completely frivolous item on graduation day. I got a good deal on the house, but not the vase."

Abe's eyes softened as he turned to his

mother. "She deserved both and more, after all those years of classes during the day and working as a nurse's aide and studying at night while raising two wild boys."

"I don't know about that—and you weren't all that wild—but this vase somehow represents a new life for me. When Vernon left us, I was terrified every day that I wouldn't be able to provide for my sons, that they'd be taken from me. But between my job, our friends, the Lord's help and the money Abe earned by mowing lawns and maintaining gardens at about a dozen homes, we stayed together. And speaking of Abe and gardens…" She gave him a mischievous grin. "If I could just get him to do one more gardening task for me, my landscaping would be done. We need to dig up my gardenia plant from the old house before it gets too late in the season to transplant it."

"Yeah, I've been meaning to do that." For a flash of a second, Abe's eyes took on that emotion she used to see on occasion, back in grade school. A raw look, as if his shame lay just below the surface.

Georgia had finished eating and wanted down, so Miss Anise lifted her from the booster seat she had gotten somewhere. As soon as her feet hit the floor, the little girl took off for the living room, and Miss Anise followed. Abe stacked the plates and carried them to the kitchen. Rosemary followed with the bowls of leftover étouffée and rice.

Putting away leftovers and washing the dishes together felt a little too much like old times, although those suppers had involved mostly bologna, hamburger and the crawfish that Abe and Jase brought from the river. Abe must have sensed it too. In the old days, he would have broken the tension by cracking a joke or intentionally misquoting a line from a movie she loved. But not today.

"You seem different tonight," she said, gentling her voice as she took a soapy plate from him and rinsed it. "I know this is hard, but it seems like something else is bothering you too."

Abe blew out a breath. "Yeah, it's hard. It's going to get harder when you and Georgia leave. But tonight I wasn't thinking about that."

He hesitated, scrubbing the next plate until its design might come off.

She didn't like the look in his eye. "What, then?"

"It's you. And Georgia. And how you live." He handed her the plate and turned to face her. "I'm guessing your dad doesn't help you. He promised me he wouldn't if we ever got together."

And Abe could probably tell by her cheap clothing and decade-old Ford Fiesta too.

"How do you get by?" he said, clenching his fist around the bunched-up dishcloth he held. "What's your home like? Because if you have to live in some run-down apartment with stained shag carpets and leaky pipes and a cheap window air conditioner that doesn't work—"

As he described his childhood home, she saw the fierce sense of protectiveness in his stance, in his tight jaw, just like the old days. "We don't. The church offered me the parsonage as a benefit. Rent-free. And it's nice."

His jaw relaxed a fraction, but he still looked as tense as he had during supper. Especially after his mother mentioned her landscaping. "What's bothering you about digging up that gardenia plant?"

He shrugged. "It's nothing."

Then she realized they had driven five or six blocks out of their way to get to his mother's house. A route that avoided his childhood home in the shabbiest part of town. "You don't ever go there, do you?"

He pulled out the sink stopper and rinsed his soapy hands. "Nope."

"But you have to get that plant."

"Wish I never had to see that again either."

He snatched a towel from the oven handle

where it hung and carried it to the drop-leaf kitchen table, drying his hands as he went. There he sank onto a Windsor chair, pitched the towel onto the table and motioned for her to join him. "I realize how stupid this sounds, but I hate that house. Sure, it was nice of JD's dad to give it to us, since he had to foreclose on ours after my dad left. But he sure picked the worst one in town. It was cheaper to give it to us than to renovate or even demolish it."

"I admit the house was pretty awful. But you and your mom fixed it up the best you could."

"I'm proud of how hard she worked to keep us together."

"But the plant…" As her voice trailed off, Rosemary prayed for wisdom. No matter what he'd done in the past, Abe was hurting—bad—and she felt a spark of compassion for him. Still, she didn't want to let down her guard.

He got up and retrieved two cans of ginger ale from the refrigerator and handed one to Rosemary. "You still like these?"

"Sure." She popped her can and took a sip.

Abe opened his but let it sit before him. "Remember our first day back at school after summer break the year Dad left? We had just moved into the shack."

That horrible day. "I remember you standing in the classroom door just before the bell rang. Some of the kids were saying their mothers had given you and Jase their hand-me-down clothes."

"And that Pastor David paid our tuition so we could keep going to our private school." As Abe gazed out the window at the lengthening early-evening shadows, some of the dusk seemed to fall in his heart, as well. "And they laughed. Talked about my dad taking off with another woman, how we lost our home. How their parents said Mama could never support Jase and me."

She waited, sensing his pain. There was more to this story than she'd known. She could feel it.

"Mama brought us to school that day. Not only to ease us into a normal routine, but also to apply for a job in the cafeteria. None of the kids knew she was there, standing right behind me. Then JD said his dad had given us a house because we were a charity case. I turned around and looked at her, and the shame in her eyes cut a hole in my heart." He hesitated, fiddling with the can. "I decided nobody would ever call us a charity case again."

It was true. She'd watched him fight that label for years, until the night he left.

"And that plant. Your grandma's friend Eldeen Rogers from the garden club brought it over that afternoon. Said it was to cheer up the place. But I knew she just wanted to see our house so she could gossip about us."

How could Rosemary have missed all this back then? Apparently, there was much more to Abe than she'd seen before. "That's another reason you need to make the gym succeed—so you can earn a good living without shame."

"Exactly. And why, despite our past, I'm thankful you're in Natchez. I need your help."

Rosemary knew what it cost him to admit that. The old Abe never would have asked for help. And this new humility looked good on him.

If only it hadn't come about four years too late.

Chapter Four

As ridiculous as it sounded, Rosemary was loving this job.

The next morning, Georgia sat at Abe's desk to color while he made a phone call there. With him watching their daughter, Rosemary focused on Mackenzie, who rolled back her chair from the receptionist desk and revealed the perfect logo for Armstrong Gym. A man and woman in workout clothes, each holding weights, a boy with a bright yellow water bottle and a ponytailed girl with a baseball bat lifted to her shoulder. Rosemary's midnight idea—getting to know Mackenzie through her social media in hopes of finding a way to reach her—had paid off. Who knew the girl sold a ton of her handmade soaps and essential oils through Etsy, and that she had a great website and a huge social media following? Apparently, everyone but

Rosemary. Gym receptionist by day and tech guru by night, Mackenzie was a marketing genius.

No wonder she was bored with answering the phone.

Even better than the fantastic new logo, Rosemary sensed this was an opportunity to draw out Mackenzie's strengths and help her to succeed at work instead of continuing to fail.

"This is a great logo. It captures everything we want to say about the gym." Especially great since Rosemary had told her only that she wanted to expand the gym's clientele to include families. "The bat is a wonderful idea, now that we're adding T-ball to the summer schedule."

Mackenzie looked down, her dark blond hair falling across her face, as if she couldn't bring herself to acknowledge Rosemary's praise.

The thought made her pause. She hadn't dreamed the girl would glow at Rosemary's approval, but she hadn't expected silence either. What kind of life had Mackenzie led before she came to Pastor David and Miss Pauline's house? How many foster homes had she been placed in, and how well had she coped?

Most important, how could Rosemary help her to leave the past behind and make the most of her life and her skills?

Then she realized how ridiculous that sounded

from a woman who hadn't yet moved on from her years-ago betrayal.

Abe emerged then from a long phone conversation in his office, leaving Georgia at his desk, coloring in the kittens-and-puppies coloring book he brought for her this morning. "What's this?"

He glanced at the screen and moved closer. Mackenzie stood and stepped aside, averting her gaze toward the weight room. She chewed the end of her pen, a slight tremor in her hand.

Did his opinion of her work mean that much to her?

Rosemary glanced back at Abe, breathing a silent prayer that he'd say the right thing.

"Mackenzie, you did this?" he asked, eyes wide, that slow grin forming on his too-handsome face. "This is fantastic!"

She nodded, still staring off into space, but her eyes took on a shine Rosemary hadn't seen before. Yes, Abe had said the right thing. He might not be the world's best businessman, but he could still sense when somebody needed help or encouragement. And somehow, he always knew how to give it.

As he'd always done for Rosemary. Tried to do the night he left, before their fight.

She'd sort of forgotten that.

"This is way better than the logo Samantha

made for us," he said. "Sam's the best worship leader in Natchez, but she's not so great at tech stuff."

Samantha... "Didn't she design your website too?"

"Yeah, and it's not the best either. You did good, Mackenzie." He held up his hand. Mackenzie hesitated a moment, then gave him a timid high five, and Abe headed toward the locker rooms. Checking them for stench again, probably.

No, Samantha wasn't the best at web design. But Rosemary was pretty sure she knew someone who was.

She sat in the extra office chair at the receptionist's desk and gestured for Mackenzie to take the seat behind the computer again. "I've noticed you doing something on your phone from time to time." An understatement, for sure. "I think you're working on something. Am I right?"

"Social media. Promoting my business."

Just as Rosemary had thought. Mackenzie hadn't been wasting time texting friends or scrolling through Instagram.

She opened the drawer closest to her, then handed Rosemary a package wrapped in lavender tissue paper and sealed with a sticker that read Magnolia Blossom Botanicals: Wisteria

Goats Milk Soap and featured an arbor covered with purple wisteria. "You can have it."

Rosemary lifted the bar, drawing in the sweet scent of wisteria. "This is too beautiful to open. But I can't help myself."

She opened the package, careful not to tear the paper or the pretty sticker, and drew out a lilac-colored bar of soap enhanced with purple petals.

"I started making little decoupage boxes for them, and I line them with soap in the shape of grass blades to make a little nest," Mackenzie said, her eyes taking on a brightness Rosemary hadn't seen before. "My customers love it. I also pad my bottles of essential oil with the soap grass."

"I'd like to see some of them. Can you bring them in tomorrow?"

"I guess."

"Good, because they'd look great on the foyer table. Want to sell some on consignment?"

"Sure. I'll package a dozen each of my most popular soaps and oils."

Rosemary hadn't expected her eager tone. In a job better suited for her, how successful could Mackenzie be? And what better place to help her start than here? "Have you seen the gym's website?"

"Uh, yeah."

"What did you think?"

Mackenzie drew a deep breath, then let it out slow. "It...needs some love."

"I looked at it last night, and I think so too. Did you create your site?"

She nodded.

"How do you like working as receptionist?"

Mackenzie hesitated. "I like Abe, and his brother is nice too. Pastor David wants me to work with them."

"But do you enjoy the work?"

"It's just that I don't always know what to say to people when they call or come in. I like opening the mail and keeping track of the payments, stuff like that."

Just as Rosemary thought. "I'm going to talk to Abe for a minute. Pull up some websites you like, and when I get back, show me some examples you think would work for the gym."

Mackenzie clicked away at the keyboard as Rosemary strode into the Armstrong Kids room. There she found a new blue tarp on the floor and blue tape covering the window and door trim. Abe came in then, carrying cans of paint and a few brushes.

"How did the locker rooms check out?" she asked.

"It smells good and all the dirty towels are out." He set down his cans and met her at the door. "How did you know Mackenzie could make logos?"

"I checked out her website. She built it herself." Rosemary slid her phone from her back pocket and pulled up Magnolia Blossom Botanicals, then handed the phone to Abe. "What do you think?"

He scrolled until he got to her picture. "This is Mackenzie's business?"

Rosemary nodded, reaching for her phone to pull up the girl's Instagram page. She gave it back to him, smiling silently at his wide-eyed stare, then drew a deep breath. "We're wasting her talent. What if we hired someone else as receptionist and made Mackenzie the gym's social media manager?"

"Go for it."

"Are you sure?"

"No question. I want to give her a job she'll succeed at." He turned back to the paint cans, got down on one knee and opened one.

Yes.

She headed to the reception area and checked out Mackenzie's website examples. Rosemary had been right about the girl's eye for marketing. She drew a deep breath, praying she was doing the right thing. "Mackenzie, how would you like to be Armstrong Gym's new social media manager?"

For the first time, she saw Mackenzie smile like a Natchez Garden Club queen.

Maybe Abe's first gift to his daughter should have been something bigger, more meaningful, than a coloring book and a box of sixty-four name-brand crayons. The kind with the built-in sharpener, just as he'd always wanted as a child. In those days, only rich kids had the big box. At least that's what his little-boy mind had thought as he'd colored with eight generic crayons, each broken in half so he and Jase could share, with his stored in a Ziploc bag so he could let Jase have the box.

Abe did have something bigger for Georgia— about ten pounds of big with huge brown eyes and a tail that never seemed to stop wagging. But what would Rosemary say? Could they take the golden retriever pup home with them? If not, Georgia would be disappointed. Then he'd have to keep him here for her to play with when they came to visit.

If they came to visit.

Come to think of it, he should probably just say the dog was his.

But since he'd bought him with Georgia in mind, he at least wanted to introduce them in a special way. A way his daughter would remember. And he didn't know a more special place in Natchez than Bluff Park.

He cleaned his paintbrush and tray and ambled up to the receptionist's desk at eleven, his stomach growling. Rosemary looked up at him with those sweet blue eyes that had kept him awake last night. Pushing aside the thought, he propped his elbow on the counter. Rosemary's lips smiled, but her eyes didn't. Great. That would keep him awake tonight too.

"Can I take you and Georgia to lunch?" he said, half expecting her to say no.

Something changed in her eyes, but he couldn't decipher the meaning. "I planned to eat at home. Daddy's at his office, so I wanted to check on Mama and fix her lunch."

She wasn't making this easy. "I was thinking about getting sandwiches and pie at the Cupboard and having a picnic on the bluff. We can take some to your mama afterward."

He caught Georgia's gaze as she grinned at him through the office window and held up her freshly colored dog picture. Then she jumped down and ran to them, carrying the book.

"All little girls love a picnic," he said. "What do you say?"

Georgia dropped the coloring book onto the floor and flung herself over Rosemary's knees.

"I want a picnic, Mama!" She rose and laid her palm against her mother's cheek. "Please?"

Rosemary sighed, smoothing the little girl's hair. "I guess."

At her lackluster response, his heart betrayed him as he remembered the way she used to bounce into his arms whenever he suggested a picnic on the bluff—her favorite thing. He tamped down his disappointment. Called himself a fool for letting the memory get to him. "I'll pick up the food and meet you at the gazebo in a half hour."

Later, having changed from his paint-spattered clothes, Abe pulled into a parking space near "their" picnic table, under a sprawling live oak. Rosemary stood with her back to him, facing their daughter and the flooded river below. Clearly uninterested in the legendary view, Georgia ran circles in the freshly mown grass. Even from the truck, he could sense Rosemary's tension in her rigid stance. He leashed the pup and set him on the ground.

Instantly whining, the puppy caught Georgia's attention, and she ran across the narrow lawn. "Mama, look. It's a puppy!"

"Georgia, stop," Rosemary called as she raced toward Georgia. "Don't run into the street."

Their daughter landed on her knees in front of the dog, giggling as the pup licked her face.

She had no more than dropped to the ground when her mother reached her.

Abe squinted in the sun, lifting his sunglasses. Had Rosemary turned pale? What was wrong with her?

"Why didn't you stop her?" Rosemary said. "She could have gotten hit."

"She stopped on her own—fifteen feet from the curb."

"Yes, but she might have kept going."

"She was just running to the dog, Rosemary," Abe said, lowering the glasses again. "She didn't get near the street."

"Okay."

Something wasn't right here. Abe might not be an expert at childcare, but even he knew that when a child hit the ground on her knees, she wasn't going to keep running toward the street. He bent down and slipped the loop of the electric-blue leash onto Georgia's wrist. "Hold on tight and walk him to the table."

"Whose dog is he?" Georgia asked.

Abe opened his mouth to say the pup belonged to him, but then he stopped. Thought a moment. "He belongs to us all. You, me and your mama."

Rosemary followed the little girl as she led the pup across the lawn. "He won't bite, will he?"

Abe blew out a breath, reaching for the Cupboard bag and drinks. "He's just a ten-week-old puppy. No, he's not going to bite."

When he reached the table and set down their meal, Georgia dropped the leash, and the pup took off for the bluff fence. Georgia ran behind him, squealing for him to stop.

Sensing that Rosemary wouldn't like her running toward the bluff any more than the street, he took off after her. Within moments, he caught her in his arms, spun her around and finally landed her on the grass to give her a belly blow. With shrieks and laughter that probably reached Pearl Street, she rolled in the lawn, playing at trying to escape.

When Abe stood and brushed off his pants, Georgia dashed over to the picnic table, the puppy toddling behind and dragging his leash with him.

Rosemary set out their glasses of blueberry lemonade and then sat down and picked up the dog, ruffling his short fur. "He's a sweet dog, Abe. Where did you get him?"

Georgia leaned over Rosemary's knee, petting the dog and talking baby talk to him.

Clearly the pup was a hit, but watching Rosemary snuggling him and Georgia giving him slobbery kisses—it did something new, something fierce to his heart. His jaw tightened as he bit back feelings he shouldn't have. Feelings he didn't deserve.

He turned away, swallowing hard to dislodge the lump growing in his throat. He'd have to deal with these renegade emotions if he hoped to make it through this meal. Through the next two weeks.

Through the rest of his life.

"I got her from Jase's boss, Miss Fannie Swan. She was looking for someone to take her dog Sunny's last pup."

Rosemary's brow creased for a moment as she looked up at him. "I thought Jase worked for you."

"He volunteers as a Rock Steady coach, and he comes in and helps out most days, but he works full-time for Miss Fannie. At her age, she can't take care of that big place of hers anymore, so he's her estate manager. Although I think a daily game of rummy is in his job description. Jase also volunteers as youth pastor at our church." Abe opened the takeout bag and pulled out their sandwiches. Then he deciphered the scribbled script on the wrapper and handed Rosemary's lunch to her. "I got you the sesame chicken salad on sourdough—the one you always liked. And grilled cheese for Georgia. I got my usual Reuben, but we can trade if you want."

That brought a smile. "I've missed their chicken salad. And Jase—with his sense of humor, I can see him working with teens. He's charming enough to win an eighty-year-old woman's loyalty too."

"He sure did. Miss Fannie treats him like a grandson. Or a great-grandson, I guess."

"What's the puppy's name?" Georgia interrupted, twisting the top off a water bottle and dousing her pink tie-dyed shorts and tennis shoes.

"He doesn't have one yet." Abe grabbed a handful of napkins and wiped water from her clothing. "Want to name him?"

Georgia danced around as he tried to wipe off more water, then gave up. "I'm gonna name him Bandit. That's Laura's dog's name."

"Who's Laura? Your friend at daycare?"

"*Little House on the Prairie* is Georgia's favorite show," Rosemary said, "and Bandit is Laura's dog."

At least his daughter hadn't wanted to call the dog Rick or Ilsa or any other reference to *Casablanca.*

After they'd eaten, Georgia begged to go to the red-roofed white gazebo overlooking the bluff, but Abe hesitated. Coming to the park was one thing. The gazebo was another.

Since he had come back, he'd avoided that

gazebo as diligently as he'd avoided their old shack. Too many memories still lingered in the white wooden structure, and Abe wasn't sure he had the strength to drive them out.

Rosemary, however, merely nodded, pulled a pack of wipes from her bag, and washed their daughter's face and hands as if the gazebo held no more meaning than the wipes did.

Fine. If it wouldn't bother her to go there, Abe could do it too. He threw their sandwich wrappers and empty bottles into the trash and gave Bandit a drink of water in the new dish Miss Fannie had sent along.

What had he been thinking, to suggest Bluff Park for a picnic? Deep down, did he want to see it again with Rosemary? No, he could honestly say he merely wanted to take Georgia to a place they had both loved.

And maybe he wanted to bring Rosemary too.

He cut that thought off cold. He had no more romantic inclinations toward her now than he had the night he left.

Before he could manage to reassure himself of the fact, Georgia and the puppy took off toward the gazebo, and Rosemary started an impromptu running game with her. Great. Now he had to watch his wife and daughter play some game he'd never heard of, that involved numbers and animal names. Their laughter and carefree hearts drove spikes into his.

Then, as soon as they got to the gazebo steps, the old memories tripped him up monumentally. Memories like the night he'd brought Rosemary here after the opening of the spring festival. It had been so late at night that no one would see them and tell the judge that Abe had dared to take a midnight walk with his beautiful daughter.

Or so they'd thought.

Then there was their wedding night.

Leaving the justice of the peace's home in Louisiana, riding Abe's motorcycle to the gazebo…

Carrying her up the gazebo steps as if it were their threshold…

He forced his mind to stop there. He couldn't let himself think about that night's kiss in the gazebo. Not with Rosemary here. Not even without her here. He'd locked up that memory for four years, and he needed to keep it that way.

"Maybe we should go." He swallowed back the huskiness he heard in his voice. "Your mom will be hungry, and we shouldn't leave her sandwich in the cooler too long."

"Right. Good idea." The flush in Rosemary's cheeks wasn't from the warmth of the late March Natchez sun. No, she remembered. It hadn't been a good memory for her either.

And they both knew Miss Cozette would be perfectly safe if she ate a roast beef sandwich that had sat in his ice-pack-filled cooler for an hour.

They needed to stay away from here. The gazebo was beyond redemption, as far as their relationship, or their nonrelationship, was concerned.

He started to turn toward the truck until Georgia's sweet little voice stopped him.

"If Bandit belongs to all three of us, that means we're a family." Georgia set her blue-eyed gaze on him. "But I don't have a daddy. Will you be the daddy?"

Her words slammed through his head, his heart, reverberating until he couldn't breathe.

At Rosemary's tiny gasp, his gaze shot to her face. But for a fraction of a moment, the old shadow of shame lurked in her eyes.

If Abe didn't know her so well, he might have missed it. It added a face slap to his daughter's gut punch. He should have realized Georgia would think she didn't have a father.

He also didn't have a prayer of pretending he didn't want her to call him Daddy.

Chapter Five

If Abe hadn't shown up looking like a special-ops soldier in his sunglasses, camo pants and close-fitting black T-shirt, Georgia's innocent words might not have ripped such a big hole in Rosemary's heart. But he had, and it stirred her repressed memory of his inner strength and self-sacrificing love, which had made her fall for him long ago. Now all she could do was continue to avoid looking at him as much as possible for the duration of this picnic-turned-disaster.

And Georgia, her little face turned up to his, hope in her eyes, wanting a daddy...

Rosemary forced a smile. "It doesn't quite work that way, Georgia."

If only she hadn't needed to say that. As soon as she had, she knew her voice sounded too light and cheerful. Abe would see right through her charade, even if her daughter didn't.

Truth was, she should have told Georgia about her father. And truth was, she'd been scared her daughter would ask to meet him. Rosemary wouldn't be able to refuse, and that could lead to the biggest heartbreak of all—Abe someday abandoning Georgia the way he'd abandoned Rosemary. But now, seeing the confusion her decision had brought to her little girl's sweet eyes, she realized her mistake. She'd have to correct it soon, but not here, where happy memories of their wedding day taunted her.

Now she just needed to get out of here.

Before she had a chance to tell Abe, Georgia let out a shriek of joy.

"Miss Anise!" Instead of taking the hand Rosemary held out to her, Georgia started jumping and pointing as she always did when she saw someone she loved. Which was everyone she met. "Mama, she's riding a Harley!"

The purring sound of a quiet motor—definitely not a Harley—drew Rosemary's attention. Sure enough, her mother-in-law pulled up to the curb and set the kickstand of the red-and-white vintage scooter Rosemary remembered from the old days.

When Georgia started for the street, Rosemary dashed to catch her. What was it about streets and vehicles that drew her daughter like an ice-cream truck? Of course, Rosemary might be a little overprotective. But Georgia was too young to understand danger, or the fact that she was the only child her worried mother would ever have, since her relationship with Abe was over and she'd never marry again.

Miss Anise removed her helmet, stashed it under the seat and pushed a wisp of hair behind her ear. As soon as her feet hit the grass, Georgia took off toward her, and Rosemary followed close. Georgia flung herself at the older woman, wrapping her arms around her legs.

Not even knowing she was hugging her grandmother.

"What do you know about Harleys, Georgia?" Abe asked, ruffling her hair and wearing a strained smile. In fact, he looked as uncomfortable as Rosemary felt.

"Mr. Kenny has one. He lets me sit on it. He has a white beard, down to here." She pointed to her own belly.

"Our neighbor," Rosemary said.

The puppy wiggled in Abe's arms, and he set him on the ground.

When the dog headed for the street, Miss Anise scooped him up and fastened his leash to a nearby bike rack. "Who is this?"

"Bandit." Georgia's eyes squinted for a moment, her lips pooching out in a little pout. "Mia's daddy got her a dog. Where's my daddy?"

The awkward silence could have driven Rosemary to tell her whole story if Miss Anise hadn't been there.

"We'll talk about it later." She looked down, hoping the others wouldn't see the flush overtaking her cheeks. "Mia is Georgia's friend from church and daycare."

"I see," Miss Anise said, and for a moment, Rosemary feared she did see—and understood—everything that had happened.

"Can I go in the little house?" Georgia said, her gaze shifting to the gazebo as a couple walked up its steps. "Please?"

Her three-year-old attention span clearly timed out, Georgia exaggerated the word, drawing it out and clasping her hands in front of her as if begging. Where had she learned to do that?

"I'll take you, if your mama doesn't mind." Miss Anise looked to Rosemary as if for permission.

The gazebo. The place she'd run to when Abe walked out…

She nodded, although it probably would have been good for Rosemary to go herself, to get it out of her system. Maybe she needed to see the familiar view of the Mississippi River and the

Natchez-Vidalia Bridge from the gazebo—and from the new perspective she'd formed over the years she'd been gone. It might help her adjust to her new normal here.

She'd do that as soon as she had that talk with Georgia about her father.

When the time was right.

Miss Anise glanced at Abe, as if asking his permission, as well. At his shrug, she reached for Bandit's leash. "Let's go see the gazebo."

Georgia, Miss Anise and Bandit ambled toward the bluff, Miss Anise holding both her granddaughter's hand and the leash. She'd be the best grandmother...

Abe turned to Rosemary, a sudden fatigue in his eyes. Clearly this was hard on him, as it would be for any man who'd always been the one to look after everyone else. Including his own mother.

"I'm sorry, Abe. If we hadn't come home, we all could have avoided a lot of pain."

But as she said the words, she knew they weren't entirely true. She would have had to tell them someday, and later might have been worse.

"It's worth it. Besides, you had to come back to Natchez." His brown eyes turned darker, more pain filled, as he and Rosemary meandered toward the river. "But we have to tell her who I am. It's great that she has you and your parents, but she has another whole family she knows nothing about. Jase hasn't asked any questions, but I'm sure he guessed, and he'll want to be part of Georgia's life. He always says that because he's adopted, family means everything to him."

"Right. I didn't mean to be selfish with her." And watching Abe interact with their daughter and help take care of her today, she'd not missed his tenderness and playfulness with her.

Standing now at the bluff fence, Rosemary took in the always breathtaking sight of the wide river two hundred feet below, its high waters rippling in the breezy afternoon, the expanse of the Natchez-Vidalia twin bridges and the rich Louisiana farmland stretched out before them. A view she'd loved her entire life. The ever-changing yet always steady Mississippi with its sunny banks and magnificent sunsets—Natchez had always been all about the river.

And so had she.

When she'd moved to the coast, she learned to love the ocean. Told herself she liked it better. But today it didn't compare to her river. The solid bluff and the never-ending current held something comforting, something lasting.

Something safe.

Rosemary waited, silent, unsure what to say to Abe. Too much, and she'd cause more pain.

Too little, and nothing would be resolved. Instead, she kept her focus on the river as she waited for Abe to speak and prayed the right words would come to them both.

"Everything I want to say seems at least a little selfish." Abe's voice grew deep and a bit ragged as he gazed out to the water. "And maybe it is. But I think every little girl needs to know who her father is."

That was true, but...

"I get that you don't want any ties to me," he said. "And I know that won't ever change. But we have a little girl over there who's more important than what you or I want."

Why did he have to be so right? And why couldn't she just say so and face her fears? "She's three years old. She'd call you Daddy no matter who's around."

Oh, that was not what she'd meant to say.

The depth of emotion in his eyes, deepening with each word she spoke, scared her. Made her think back to the time she'd seen it last—the day he'd given her his ultimatum. And left when she'd defied it.

"I'm not saying you're wrong. But let me think about it, Abe."

And then, in that special-ops-soldier way he had, he nodded once and turned from her, leaving her wishing for something she couldn't name, something even her river couldn't give.

For the rest of the day, Abe wandered around the local home-improvement store, pretending he needed to know every detail about all the plumbing supplies and child-size bathroom fixtures for the Armstrong Kids room. In reality, he was dawdling because he dreaded facing Rosemary again. During his four years away from his hometown, a thin scab had started to form over his raw wounds, as well as the old ones. His success in the army, starting a new business and reconnecting with Mama and Jase had helped some too. But just one look from Rosemary at the bluff—that look that said, "I'm still ashamed of you"—and bam. He was back in that shack. Or in that school hallway. Not really good enough to be with the rest of the kids but tolerated because they felt sorry for him.

A charity case.

Back at the gym at five thirty, he spent a half hour working out and then headed up the stairs to his apartment. He'd improved it, for sure, adding tongue-and-groove wood flooring, a great kitchen with stone countertops and new appliances, and a luxury bath. Still, who was he kidding? He wanted to be in Georgia's life, but what mother wanted her little girl to visit her father in an apartment over a gym full of sweaty guys?

Then again, there weren't that many guys there, and not that much sweat...

Especially since Rosemary hired the new cleaning crew.

His phone buzzed, and he checked his texts. Mama, reminding him it was family night at her house.

Of all nights.

He texted back, offering to pick up banana caramel pie at the Cupboard, and hit the shower.

When he got to Mama's Orleans Street house, carrying the Cupboard's famous banana pie, a red '67 Mustang convertible sat in the driveway.

Who did they know with a sweet ride like that?

Inside, the house smelled of Cajun shrimp and Mama's good fresh bread. He headed toward the sound of her voice and Jase's in the kitchen, eager to discover who owned the Mustang. But when he got there, he found only his mother shaking her shrimp-filled iron skillet over the fire while Jase added shredded cheese to the salad. Just like old times, when Abe always came home late from his mowing and weed-pulling jobs after school, and Mama and Jase were in the kitchen, cooking supper.

Abe glanced around the kitchen and looked into the dining room. "Do we have company?"

Mama smiled, a twinkle in her eye. "It's just us tonight."

"Then whose Mustang is that?" He looked out the window to the driveway, then back to his mother. She wore her blond waves down tonight, looking more like a mother of junior high kids than a parent of two grown men. "It's yours, isn't it? You traded in your Jeep?"

Couldn't be. She never let the Jeep—or her scooter—sit outside.

"Guess again," she said.

Then who—

His brother pulled a set of keys from his pocket and jingled them in front of Abe's face.

Jase bought a Mustang?

"What? No! I will not allow my little brother to have a cooler vehicle than mine."

"Then you'd better get to a car dealership."

Mama laughed, playfully swatting Jase's hand and the keys. "Tell him the whole story."

Jase pocketed the keys. "Well, it might belong to Miss Fannie."

"Miss Fannie has a Mustang?" This was even less believable.

"It belonged to her late husband, Colonel Chester. He's been dead so long, I think she forgot she had it, stored away in the old carriage house with the other vehicles."

"How did you end up with it?" Abe asked, tamping down a surge of jealousy.

"I think she wants me to have a better image as her employee. Or she's tired of my eighteen-year-old Taurus sitting around. Anyway, she wants me to drive it."

More likely, it was a perk to make up for Jase's small salary. And he deserved it, the way he served the elderly woman. "Take me for a drive later."

When they'd sat down and said grace, Abe realized the time had come to tell his brother about Georgia, although Jase was smart enough to have figured it out already. Still, they couldn't tiptoe around the facts forever. He drew a deep breath, trying to sound natural while he scooped shrimp onto his plate. "Jase, I need to tell you something. That little girl with Rosemary at boxing class—she's my daughter. Mine and Rosemary's."

Jase grunted. "Yeah, I wondered when you'd get around to bringing that up."

He probably deserved that. It'd been two days already. "Sorry. It took me some time to get used to it myself."

"You didn't know?" His brother's eyes had grown wide.

"I found out Georgia existed about five minutes before you did."

Jase laid down his fork. "Dude, I'm sorry. Ever since that day, I've been trying to figure this thing out. I knew you weren't the kind of man to leave town with your girlfriend pregnant, but that's kind of what it looked like."

No, he'd left town with his wife pregnant. Which was worse, in a way.

"I also couldn't figure out how this happened," Jase said, "because you were always telling me to wait for marriage because that was what you were going to do. I guess you left that way of thinking behind."

He'd expected the disappointment in his brother's tone. Wow, he'd let more people down than he'd realized. And even though Abe had kept his years-ago vow to wait, he couldn't tell his brother. Couldn't erase Jase's feeling of betrayal, since he'd promised Rosemary to keep their marriage secret.

"You two need to talk about this alone. I'm going to finish my supper on the back gallery." Mama pushed back her chair and picked up her plate and fork. "Jason, try not to make your brother feel bad about this. What's done is done."

Abe didn't try to stop her, since she looked a little uncomfortable with the conversation.

When the door closed behind her and her chair scraped across the gallery's wooden floor, Jase grimaced—or was he trying to smile? "She must mean it, since she used my whole name."

"Yeah." At least she hadn't called him Abraham when he brought Rosemary and Georgia over here, although she'd had good reason to. "I wish—"

He hesitated. He wished what? That he hadn't married Rosemary? He had at first, but the years had mellowed that feeling. That they didn't have Georgia? Never. "I wish I could explain the whole situation."

"You're my brother. You don't owe me anything." Jase held up his hand. "Besides, I've been in the ministry since you left town. I've heard all kinds of explanations."

Not like this one.

"And I'm keeping my commitment to waiting, regardless."

Abe would have given his Bronze Star if he could have told Jase the truth—that he'd kept his too.

Chapter Six

Every little girl needs to know who her father is. Abe's words from yesterday rolled through Rosemary's mind the next morning as she made breakfast for her family. He was right. She couldn't keep the truth from her daughter any longer. Today Rosemary would set aside her fear, as much as she could, and do what was right for Georgia. And for Abe. Hopefully, by the end of the day, she and Abe would set a time to let her daughter know she has a daddy.

As she took the biscuits from the oven, her father came to breakfast in his black pinstripe suit, white shirt and charcoal tie, the knot a little lopsided. "I need a ride to the courthouse after breakfast."

Then why was he wearing his suit? He'd be at work only an hour before they had to leave for boxing class, and with the progression of his Parkinson's, it often took him almost half an hour to change clothes.

She turned off the heat under her pan of scrambled eggs and flipped the fried potatoes. "You could wear casual clothes to work and then change into your suit after the boxing class."

"I have an early court case. Natchez has seen me wearing a suit under my robes every day for the past thirty years, and they're going to see me wearing a suit today."

"Nobody in your court cares what you wear to work." She checked the potatoes. Nice and crisp, just as her father liked. She spooned them into Great-Grandmother Eloise's hyacinth Spode serving dish.

As she set them on the table, she caught a glimpse of her father watching her. Not to make sure she made the potatoes and biscuits to his liking, but something deeper. Something she'd recognized only once before—when he'd caught her and Abe kissing in the gazebo after the spring festival.

Why had Daddy seen her first two kisses? She could understand him looking for her when she and Cody Lewis disappeared during her thirteenth birthday party. But why had he followed her and Abe to the gazebo that night?

They were just kisses, nothing more. What

had he been afraid of? Why hadn't he trusted her? Why didn't he trust her now?

But maybe she wasn't the one he didn't trust. Maybe he didn't trust boys—and now men—in general.

For the same reason she was afraid to tell Georgia that Abe was her father.

Mama came in from the sitting room, where Rosemary had left her reading her daily devotional a half hour ago. "Burley, you can't wear that today."

"Is there a law against wearing a suit to boxing class?"

"No, but you can't box in a suit," Mama said as if she knew what she was talking about. "And they won't let you on the basketball floor in those shoes."

He looked down at his feet. "I'd rather go to work than bounce a ball and hit a punching bag. That's not going to do me any good."

Rosemary had known Daddy would eventually put up a fight about Rock Steady Boxing classes. But she hadn't expected it quite this soon.

She hesitated, choosing her words carefully. "The sparring, footwork and punching-bag routines are supposed to be the perfect exercises to slow the effects of Parkinson's. Look how it's helping Pastor David."

Her father got up and headed toward their bedroom in the back of the house. "You'd just better hope Abe Armstrong is never my sparring partner."

An hour later, Rosemary and Georgia pulled up to the gym after dropping off Daddy, who wore khakis, a polo shirt and tennis shoes, at the courthouse. Georgia pointed out the window. "There's Grannie's golf cart."

Sure enough, the cart, decorated with garden club decals and silk replicas of the town's famous crepe myrtles, sat in the Natchez Coffee Shop parking lot. Rosemary smiled. No doubt she was arranging a meeting between Rance and some unknown, possibly unsuspecting, lady.

Grannie Eugenia, the resident matchmaker. Who knew? And if Grannie was so good at fanning romances into flame, why couldn't Rosemary figure out her own problems of the heart? Probably because it was easier to start a new relationship than it was to fix a broken one. Not that she could fix her beyond-broken relationship with Abe, even if she wanted to. That romance was shattered into as many pieces as the rocks in the Mississippi River.

However hopeless their romance, she could do something about another relationship: Abe and Georgia's. He was right. Their daughter needed to know he was her father, and they didn't have much time to do it. Aunt Anjohnette would be here soon, then Rosemary and Georgia would leave for the island, with no plans to return.

They needed to make time to talk, soon. Today.

Inside the gym, a woman waited in the foyer, wearing upscale workout clothes and high-dollar athletic shoes, her straight, dark hair in a high ponytail. Fit and stylish, she stood and held out her hand.

Could this be Rosemary's nine-o'clock receptionist interview?

"Ms. Williams? I'm Lauren Slater." She seemed about Rosemary's age and somehow looked confident and professional, even in workout clothes. "I knew it was you because Mr. Armstrong told me to watch for a woman with a little girl who looked just like her."

"I'm Rosemary Williams. We use first names here." A full thirty minutes early, this beauty made a great first impression. Rosemary shook Lauren's hand, taking in her wide smile and pretty green eyes. Then she checked her left hand and, finding a wedding ring and a huge diamond in her engagement ring, she drew a breath of relief.

She glanced toward the under-construction

Armstrong Kids room and saw Abe installing the new carpet. He looked up and waved, and she instantly shook away the envy she'd nearly indulged in. Why had it mattered that Lauren looked like a model? Why would it matter if she were single? And why would it matter if Abe recognized how gorgeous Lauren was? Rosemary had no right to jealousy, because although they were married, they had no marriage.

And while Rosemary had held fast to her conviction of not filing for divorce, there was always the possibility that Abe would find someone else and file.

Why had she thought of that today, after all these years of refusing to let herself wonder when divorce papers would come in the mail?

Whatever the reason, if she could refrain from thinking about it before, she could do it again now.

Before the ten-o'clock boxing class started, she had hired Lauren as receptionist and changed the gym's dress code to workout clothes for all staff.

Daddy's intern, Olivia, dropped him off, and he shuffled toward the basketball court with Georgia. Seeing them together, Rosemary stepped into the Armstrong Kids room to talk to Abe. Today he wore an old pair of jeans and a navy blue Ole Miss T-shirt, fitted enough to accentuate those muscular shoulders and biceps.

Well.

Who knew a college football shirt could look as good as a tux?

He finished sweeping the new carpet and turned off the vacuum.

"Do you still like to watch Mississippi football?" she asked.

"What do you think?" he asked, grinning as he wrapped the cord around the vacuum. "Do you?"

"Sometimes." She turned her focus to the floor. "You're doing a great job with this room. Can we bring in the furniture and toys this afternoon?"

"That's the plan. The bathroom and kitchenette fixtures should be finished tomorrow too. We're on target to open this room next week." He leaned against a cabinet, his arms crossed in front of him.

Even though she'd already made up her mind to have that talk with Georgia, she felt awkward. "This is hard for me to say, so I'm just going to come out and say it. I'd like for us to spend some time together with Georgia and tell her about you. But I don't want a quick conversation and then we each go home. I think she needs time with both of us to get used to the idea."

"Yeah." He rubbed the back of his neck as if the muscles had suddenly tightened. "Let's do that. When and where?"

"I could make a picnic lunch tomorrow," she said. "We could drive out to Melrose. Georgia wouldn't be interested in the house museum, but we could eat there anyway like we used to. Do they still have picnic tables behind the old mansion?"

"Jase will know. I'll check with him."

Rosemary caught a glimpse of Mackenzie waving through the window wall from her station at the reception desk and then pointing at the computer monitor. Grateful for the distraction from this strained conversation, she waved back. "Mackenzie should have the new website finished by now. Want to come and look at it before boxing class?"

He checked his watch. "Sure. We have about five minutes. The boxers started pulling up a while ago."

When they reached Mackenzie's desk, the girl seemed almost to glow as she scrolled through the pages for them, pointing out features she'd included.

"I tried to make it contemporary but not strictly youth oriented," Mackenzie said. "Rosemary, your grandma brought in two of her friends today to join the gym. I told them you were thinking of starting a seniors' stretching class, and they loved the idea. Talking to them, I realized I needed to make seniors feel comfortable on the site too."

"Good thinking," Abe said. "And you did a great job with this site. Go ahead and publish it."

"Yes!" Mackenzie pumped her fist in the air.

Rosemary couldn't help grinning as she and Abe headed toward the gym, just minutes before Daddy's second boxing class started. "Will this class be the same as Tuesday's?" she asked, remembering her father's complaints about Rock Steady Boxing at breakfast.

"Some things are the same. We always warm up before we do balance and cognitive exercises and then go into the boxing room. But sometimes we add a special activity, like today."

A special activity sounded nice. "What is it?"

Abe gave her a teasing grin. "Today we teach your father how to fall without getting hurt."

For the first time, Rosemary saw Georgia in his smile, and it both warmed and pierced her heart. She could only hope that, after Georgia learned she had a father, their little girl wouldn't get hurt.

Great. Abe was about to become the laughingstock of Natchez. No, make that the laughingstock of southern Mississippi.

"Speaking in public isn't my thing. This is going to be terrible." For a man who'd led a team of a dozen men into the minefields of Afghanistan, talking on the radio should be a breeze. But it wasn't. His troops had known him, supported him. Whatever he said, they did. But radio? Talking to people he couldn't even see? The thought shot shrapnel into his heart.

"You'll be fine," Rosemary said in that soothing voice of hers as she and Georgia waited with him for the radio station to call. "I'll stay here across the desk from you, and you can just talk to me instead of thinking about the radio audience. They won't even know I'm here."

He shrugged. Here he was in his office, waiting for the phone to ring, and then Rosemary and the news guy at WQNZ expected him to answer it and start talking about the gym and Rock Steady Boxing. And Rosemary would be there, silently cheering him on like the woman of grace she was.

Then, before he knew it, it was ten minutes till four, and the phone rang.

His mouth suddenly dry, he drew a blank. What had he decided to say? He grabbed the list of interview questions he and Rosemary had put together and scanned the first one and its answer.

"Caller ID says it's WQNZ," she said, sliding

the desk phone a little closer. Then, clearly expecting him to answer it, she turned to Georgia and smiled at her, her finger on her own lips as if this were a game. "Be as quiet as you can, and color in the coloring book Mr. Abe gave you. He's going to talk on the radio."

At his daughter's giggle, Abe reached for the phone, answered and made small talk with Colin, the news guy, who sounded like a high school kid.

"We'll go live in thirty seconds," Colin said and then started a countdown every five seconds.

Finally he introduced Abe to the invisible audience, and Abe read the opening line Rosemary had written in his notes.

"Your Rock Steady Boxing classes help people with Parkinson's. Tell us a little about the program and how it helps them."

Abe stumbled through the answer they'd written, sounding wooden, even to his own ears. This was going terrible already. The interview was supposed to last ten minutes, and he'd managed to botch up the first fifteen seconds. How was he going to get through this?

"I've heard you have a partner working with you on the new RSB program and the gym renovations. Is that true?"

An impromptu question…no…

Colin had apparently sensed his nervousness and thought asking a question of his own would loosen Abe up a little. But he was wrong.

Instead of answering, Abe fumbled for words. Any words. The listeners could probably hear his thudding heartbeat through their speakers.

About the time he was considering hanging up, Rosemary pushed the speaker button. "This is Rosemary Williams, Abe's..."

Why the hesitation? He swiped at the sweat on his brow.

"Consultant."

Consultant. Yes. He managed a thumbs-up in her direction.

"Tell us a little about your experience with Rock Steady Boxing, Rosemary."

"Sure. Abe's mentor had been diagnosed with Parkinson's a few years ago, and he wasn't doing so well. So Abe started this program, and Pastor David started fighting back against Parkinson's, as we say. The exercises improved his quality of life by lessening his tremors and stiffness and improving his agility and gait, among other things. The camaraderie is amazing too."

Abe detected the note of sweetness in her voice, could even hear the smile in it, and he was sure the listeners could too. As she chatted on about how RSB had helped Pastor David and what the class could do for people with Parkinson's, it was plain to see she was great at this.

"Since my father's first day at boxing class, I've been his corner person, and my three-year-old daughter, Georgia, has become the team mascot."

"I'll bet the boxers love her. Georgia, if you're listening, WQNZ Radio says thank you for helping the boxers get stronger."

Georgia stood up in her chair and leaned close to the phone speaker. "You're welcome!"

Colin laughed while Rosemary held their daughter steady. "So little Georgia is there with you?"

"I'm here," she said.

"Well, sweetheart, how do you like boxing class?"

"It's fun. You get to bounce balls and hit a punching bag and fall down."

"Fall down?" Colin asked, exaggerated concern in his voice, apparently for Georgia's benefit. "I hope nobody got hurt."

"Nope. Mr. Abe said, 'Judge Williams, I'm gonna teach you how to fall down and not get hurt.' And Mama said, 'No, you're not. He's gonna break his neck.' And Mr. Abe whispered, real quiet so Grampa couldn't hear, and he said, 'That ole bird is too stubborn to get hurt.' And he didn't."

Abe choked back a groan. Now the judge would hold Abe's stubborn-bird comment against him. Then again, what was one more grievance on top of the hundred or so he already had?

When Colin stopped laughing, Abe said, "Falls can be a big problem, since Parkinson's affects the gait and balance. So we use a gymnastics mat to teach them to fall more safely and hopefully prevent injuries."

Rosemary smiled encouragement, and he realized the words had come easily this time. Probably because he'd worked hard to learn methods to prevent falls and injuries after Pastor David started having problems. Or simply because Georgia had taken his mind off himself.

Nearing the end of the ten minutes, Rosemary highlighted the new programs they were starting and the new Armstrong Kids room, and then he gave instructions for joining the Rock Steady Boxing class. At the end, as they were hanging up, Georgia cheered, "Rock Steady Boxing!" as if they'd rehearsed it all week.

When Abe hung up the phone, he took his little girl in his arms and gave her a hug. "You did a good job, Georgia. I'm proud of you."

Rosemary reached across the table and squeezed his hand. "You did great, too, Abe. Once you got started, you were a natural."

He cleared his suddenly dry throat, savoring the feel of her hand in his, smelling her orange-blossom perfume, like back in the old days…

The phone rang.

He pulled his hand away.

"It's Colin again," Rosemary said, checking the caller ID, her cheeks flushing a beautiful pink.

Abe's face felt a little heated too. He lifted the receiver and punched the line and speaker buttons. "Armstrong Gym."

"The phones went wild during the broadcast, and they're still lit up."

"You're kidding me, Colin. I was a dud."

"Sorry, but you weren't the star of the show, buddy. The whole town of Natchez is calling in to say they love the little girl, and they want to hear more from her. Let's schedule another interview, and then we'll set up those info-blurbs we talked about. Three times a week, not just once like we originally planned. If people keep calling, we might increase to daily."

Abe grinned, glancing at Rosemary, who had covered her mouth with her hand. Her eyes betrayed her smile, though.

"Well, it's settled. I've been overshadowed by my own—"

He caught himself just in time. Rosemary's face paled.

"My own consultant's daughter," he finished, looking away. "Georgia would do a great job, but she and her mother are leaving soon for their home on St. Simons Island."

"That's a shame. They loved her, and you and Ms. Williams had some great chemistry going on too. Y'all are a great team." Colin's voice held a note of disappointment. "What if we record some clips before she goes? It'll help our ratings plus give you some great exposure for your gym."

Abe looked at Rosemary for her reaction. She merely shrugged.

"Colin, I'll get back with you."

"Do me a favor and talk Rosemary into staying in Natchez."

When Abe hung up, he realized for the first time how lonely this gym would be once they were gone. Rosemary and Georgia had rescued him from being the laughingstock of Natchez, for sure. And he couldn't help but wonder what life would be like if Rosemary decided to stay.

He pushed aside the thought. She had no reason to stay. Her life, Georgia's life, was on the island. And they'd turned his life upside down when they showed up in his gym. He was beginning to understand Rosemary's concern that Georgia would get too attached to him, and that the little girl would be hurt when they left.

Abe would have to guard his heart. It would be way too easy to selfishly try to give Rosemary a reason to stay.

Chapter Seven

The gym's new receptionist might have influenced Rosemary more than she wanted to admit.

Returning to her parents' house after a three-mile run early the next morning, she limped up the front steps to the gallery, her calves aching. What had made her think running was a good idea? She'd been one of the least athletic students in gym class all through her school years, and the fact had never bothered her before. But now she had to stay healthy in order to take care of Georgia.

Oh, who was she trying to kid? She had to face the truth, if only to herself. Lauren Slater, looking as if she already lived in a gym, had made Rosemary feel a little too curvy yesterday afternoon at her receptionist orientation. So this morning, she'd decided to do something about it. Granted, her "run" was more like a walk with a little bounce in her step. But it was a start. And if Abe could keep himself looking dangerously handsome, well, she could improve herself a little too.

She kicked off the running shoes she bought last night, pitched them against the wall and flopped down on one of the wooden benches on the gallery. She took a moment to rub her aching feet, even though she needed to get back to the kitchen and the breakfast she'd prepped before her run. Daddy would be grumpier than ever if he didn't get his made-from-scratch breakfast.

How had Mama managed all this cooking plus taking care of their enormous house by herself after working at the historical society every day and as president of the Natchez Garden Club? It was probably time to hire some housekeeping help until Mama's arm healed. They'd recently closed off the north wing, but that still left twelve rooms to clean, including Grannie's wing. Rosemary didn't mind spending her evenings cleaning and doing laundry, but Aunt Anjohnette, ten years older than Mama, wouldn't be able to keep up with that schedule once she arrived and Rosemary and Georgia went home.

And how would Abe keep up without Rosemary's help? She'd been here five days now, and she had just over a week left before she had to go back to her job on the island. Would her efforts in that short time be enough? And the thought that had been pricking her mind every night: What if Rock Steady Boxing didn't help her father? Aunt Anjohnette had her own home in Vicksburg. She couldn't stay and help him indefinitely.

Maybe they all were expecting the boxing class to deliver healing only the Lord could provide.

Groaning a little, she leaned over, picked up her shoes and headed for the front door. Inside, she heard a sound in the sitting room and turned toward it.

There sat her father and Georgia, playing Go Fish on the Hepplewhite end table they'd apparently pulled up to Daddy's great-great-grandmother's pink damask sofa. Georgia drew a card from his hand and laid down a pair of twos.

Her father smiled.

It was a tiny smile, but his eyes twinkled a bit, as well.

He looked up from his hand. "She's beating me, Rosemary."

Her heart lurched, and the sting of tears in her eyes almost kept her from seeing him smile again. She covered her mouth with her hand, her breath coming fast. She'd thought Parkinson's had stolen her father's smile forever.

How long had it been since she'd seen any expression on his face? A year? Two? She had no idea what could have brought this change. Except boxing class.

Was that even possible? He'd gone only twice. It seemed incredible, but what other change had he made? His prescription dosages hadn't increased in six months. He wasn't doing anything else differently.

Rosemary turned and headed for the kitchen, not wanting her father to see her tears. There she splashed water on her face and took some deep breaths. She'd had no idea how much she'd missed his expressions, but she knew she was grateful. "Thank You, Lord. I don't know how long this will last, but thank You for letting me see his smile again."

Georgia burst into the room then, a big grin on her face. "I beat Grampa at Go Fish," she said, holding up a fistful of cards. "He wants to know why Mr. Abe said he's a stubborn ole bird. Grampa says he's not stubborn at all."

Apparently, her father's new changes didn't include facing reality about his personality.

Hours later, after a morning spent working in Mama's prized flower beds, Rosemary grabbed a quick shower and then stood, in her summer robe, inside her closet. It hurt a little to look at the clothes Mama had left hanging there. Her favorite jeans, a few shirts, her prom dresses. Not to mention all the pageant costumes she'd worn through the years, including the white gown she wore the spring she was the garden club queen, and Abe was the king.

That was another night she wished she could erase from her memory.

Then she spotted her special light blue "I'm just a muffaletta; everybody loves me" T-shirt, the one Abe bought for her in Jackson Square during their senior class trip to New Orleans. She'd worn it while she and Abe ate muffalettas, sitting at the back counter of Central Grocery the last night of their trip. On their first and only actual date that didn't involve sneaking around to keep her father from finding out.

She pulled the shirt from its hanger and slipped it over her head. Then she slid into her jeans and front-tucked the shirt. It looked cute and casual, and she was tempted to wear it for their picnic today. Abe wouldn't remember it, so she might as well. No need to continue to keep it for sentiment's sake.

Rosemary slipped into her sandals and pulled her hair into a low ponytail, then she headed to the kitchen and made chicken salad sandwiches with extra-sharp cheddar and butter-crunch lettuce from the garden. She stashed them in the cooler along with Abe's favorite: marinated cherry tomatoes with fresh basil and feta. Since the tomatoes' flavor was too strong for Georgia, she also tucked in a package of string cheese and some baby carrots.

She glanced at the kitchen clock. Ten minutes till twelve. Rosemary started through the main house, calling for Georgia, but the little girl didn't answer. After a quick check of their bedrooms, Rosemary ran down the stairs and into Grannie's wing. There she found her daughter and grandmother on Grannie's four-poster walnut bed, looking at an old photo album.

"Mama, look. It's you and Mr. Abe."

Sure enough, the picture showed Rosemary in her white gown and Abe in his borrowed suit, ready for the pageant's opening night five years ago. How could so much love shine from their eyes in a years-old picture?

Then she noticed a similar picture on the album's opposite page. It was Mama and Vernon Armstrong—Abe's father—in front of the decades-old pageant backdrop the year they were king and queen. She'd seen that picture a dozen times, but the one below it made her catch her breath. "Grannie, this looks like—is it a prom picture? Of Mama and Vernon?"

"Their senior year. It's the only existing copy of this picture."

Rosemary sank down onto the bed next to her

grandmother, the truth sinking in. "But Mama said their senior prom picture was lost."

"Of course it was. To them. Your father was threatening to burn it one night when he was in a jealous rage, and I sneaked into the attic and rescued it."

"But that means Mama and Vernon...dated."

How had Rosemary never heard? None of this made sense. "Why haven't you told me this before?"

"Because your mother asked me not to."

"But why show me the picture now?"

"I didn't. You happened in here when I had the album out, and you discovered for yourself that Vernon and your father were once rivals for your mother's love."

"You didn't try to hide it, though."

Her grandmother sighed, something Rosemary rarely heard her do. "It's time this secret came out. This is why your father objected to you and Abe dating."

Rosemary closed her eyes, letting this new revelation sink in. Surely Grannie knew what she was talking about, and it explained a lot. Daddy must have been furious. Or deeply hurt.

Or both.

Grannie turned the page as if turning the conversation, as well. She pointed to the next picture. "I love this one of you, Rosemary. You're wearing the shirt you have on now."

Abe had taken it, the Cabildo in the background.

"You glow in this picture."

Sure she did. Abe had given her the kiss of a lifetime ten seconds before he snapped it. "Time to go, Georgia," she said, holding out her hand. "Grannie, I'm sorry to take her away from you. Let's play a game of Old Maid together in the sitting room tonight."

Grannie gave her that same look she'd had when she told Rosemary about her matchmaking schemes. "I'll play the game with you and Georgia, but I don't like the phrase 'old maid.' It's disrespectful and it's against my principles to allow any woman to remain unmarried, if she wants a husband. Keep that in mind if the Armstrong boy holds out too long."

Rosemary cleared her throat, stalling in order to come up with a gracious answer and tone. "I'll let you know if I need help."

"Good. And if Mr. Armstrong is still hungry after eating your chicken salad, stop at the Cupboard. They have red beans and rice today. All men love red beans and rice."

What? How did Grannie know she was meeting Abe today, and how did she know about the chicken salad? "If I didn't know better, I'd think you've been reading my text messages."

Her grandmother laughed. "No, and I haven't been hovering around, eavesdropping on your conversations either. I called the gym to make an appointment with him to discuss my ideas for senior classes, and he said he couldn't meet me at noon because he was going on a picnic. Since men don't picnic alone or with other men, he had to be going with you, because they say he hasn't looked at a woman since he got home from the army. At least until you came home."

Rosemary chose to ignore her last sentence. "And the chicken salad?"

"Simple. Your father dislikes it, so your mother never keeps it in the house. It had to be yours. And everybody knows chicken salad is perfect picnic food. For a woman."

"Meaning?"

Grannie reached for her hand and squeezed it for a moment. "A man generally prefers a thick ham or roast beef sandwich. But he'll eat chicken salad without complaining if it comes from the hand of the woman he loves. I know your young man, and I know you're perfect together. I want to see you both happy."

Rosemary sighed. "It's a whole lot more complicated than that."

Her grandmother gazed pointedly at Rosemary's muffaletta shirt as if she knew its history. "It's just about as complicated as you make it."

Ten minutes later, she pulled up beside Abe's truck in Melrose's parking lot and helped Georgia out of the car. Abe stood leaning against the truck, the puppy nipping at the hems of his jeans.

"Mr. Abe, you brought Bandit to our picnic," Georgia squealed, dropping to her knees in the grass and throwing her arms around the dog's neck.

"He wanted to see you." Abe gave her the leash, and she ran across the expansive yard with the puppy. He turned to Rosemary. "I'd forgotten what a great spot this is."

Rosemary managed a smile. "She'll always remember it as the place where she gained a father."

He hesitated, then popped the trunk and reached for the cooler. "I'll always be that to her. I won't let her down."

For the first time, she glimpsed a shred of hope.

As soon as they all started toward the picnic area behind the house museum, near its many outbuildings, Rosemary caught Abe looking at her, at her shirt, in the shade of the giant live oaks around them.

"New Orleans," he said, his voice soft, steady. Rosemary sucked in a breath. "Yeah."

She should have known he'd remember. What had she been thinking, wearing this shirt? It had been such a happy time for them, and maybe she'd just wanted something positive between them for a change...

"That was one of the best times of my life," he said. "Away from my shack of a house, away from your father—it was almost like we were normal people with normal lives."

"I felt that way too." She hadn't viewed her life the same since, not really. Because how many people's lives turned out the way hers had? Being away from home with Abe, knowing she loved him and confident of his love for her, she'd somehow changed that week. Without realizing it, she'd begun to see herself and Abe as a couple, but not a typical teen couple. She started to believe they'd be together forever, that she would help him succeed in his landscaping business and he would help her become a teacher. They'd be a team, working together and loving each other for the rest of their lives.

For the first time since he left her, she wished that feeling would come back.

Today Abe would do the thing his father had never done. He would promise his child that he'd always be here for her. And he would begin his lifetime commitment to Georgia. No matter what, she would have a father as long as he was alive. He hadn't yet figured out how to navigate the distance between their homes, but he would. If he had to sell his gym and move to St. Simons Island, he'd do it.

If Rosemary would agree.

Georgia scrambled over to the nearest live oak and found a limb low enough to sit on. She chattered and sang there, petting Bandit and brushing her palms over the Spanish moss growing on her seat.

Abe spread Rosemary's pretty flowered cloth over the table's rough boards while she wiped the seats. In a way, it felt like the old days, when they'd had to sneak around and have picnics in more remote areas so the judge wouldn't find out they were together. Today she looked cute in her jeans and T-shirt. But he remembered how she'd taken his breath away all those years ago, sitting at this table and wearing a light yellow dress that made her face all but glow.

Did she remember too? Maybe, since she'd suggested another picnic so soon after the one that had gone wrong at the bluff. And since she'd chosen the same secluded table he'd picked out for them that night.

Or maybe she'd forgotten that special night,

and they'd both just subconsciously reverted to their old ways.

When they'd set out the food and drinks, plates and silverware, and Abe had secured the puppy's leash to the table leg, he bowed his head to pray. Then he changed his mind and held out his hand to Georgia. She took it and lowered her head, closing her eyes and looking like the sweetest little girl ever born. He swallowed back the burning in his throat. He didn't deserve this sacred moment with his daughter. He didn't even deserve to have a child like Georgia.

He did the only thing he could think of. Reaching across the table, he held out his hand to Rosemary, hoping she'd understand what he couldn't say—that they needed the help of the Savior if they were going to make this work. Abe had messed up everything so much that he could never keep the vows he was about to make to Georgia unless he had the Lord's help.

She hesitated, then clasped his hand quickly, as if she was afraid she might change her mind if she didn't do it immediately.

That was okay with him. It was a start.

When he'd said "Amen" and raised his head, Georgia kept hers bowed. "Jesus, bless Mama and Mr. Abe. Amen."

At the sound of his daughter praying for him,

that burning in his throat started all over again and somehow spread to his eyes.

As Rosemary filled Georgia's plate, he took a long gulp of water to soothe his throat.

He reached for the tomato salad and spooned a big helping onto his plate. One thing was sure: Rosemary knew how to cook. And she must have remembered he liked it. The chicken salad didn't look like it came from the Cupboard. He took a bite. It was even better than the Cupboard's.

Rosemary caught his eye and gave him a little nod, as if encouraging him to start the conversation he both anticipated and dreaded.

"Georgia," he said, a little surprised that she wanted him to be the one to bring it up. "Do you remember asking your mother a question the day we went to the river bluff?"

She pulled her brows into a frown as if thinking hard.

"About your daddy," Rosemary said, her gaze fixed on their daughter as if afraid she might start to cry or something.

"I remember." She nodded vigorously enough to make her high ponytail bounce.

"I think it's time to tell you about him," Rosemary said.

"Okay." Their daughter took a giant bite of

her sandwich. Apparently the urgency of having a father had worn off.

"Georgia, look at me." Rosemary laid her finger under the girl's chin and gently turned her face toward her. "I want to tell you who your daddy is."

"Okay. Who?"

Rosemary drew a deep breath, looking as anxious as Abe was beginning to feel. "Mr. Abe is your daddy."

"No, he's not."

Rosemary's gaze shot to his. Didn't Georgia want him for her father?

"What makes you think that?" Rosemary said.

"He don't live with us." She crammed another bite into her mouth and spoke around it. "Mia's daddy lives with her and her mama."

Rosemary blew out a breath. "Some daddies live with their children, and others don't."

Georgia turned her blue-eyed gaze to his and held it there so long, Abe began to squirm. Did she think he didn't want to live with her? Or that he didn't want her at all?

How was he supposed to explain this?

"Mr. Abe lives here in Natchez, and we live on St. Simons Island," Rosemary said.

"Can we move here?" she asked.

"I have my job on the island."

"Then Mr. Abe can move there too."

"No, because his job is here. And his mother, Miss Anise, is here."

Georgia wasn't buying this flimsy explanation—Abe could sense it. "Honey, I'm your daddy, but I didn't know it until you came to Natchez. If I had known, I would have come to see you sooner."

She wrinkled her brow again. "How come you didn't know?"

This conversation was getting way deeper than Abe was willing to go. "It just happens that way sometimes. But I'm your daddy, and I'm going to take care of you. If you need anything, I'll get it for you. And if you need me, I'll fly right out to St. Simons Island and be there for you."

"Promise?"

Oh, those eyes. "I promise. You'll always have a daddy."

Georgia heaved a huge sigh. "I guess so, but it's not gonna feel like it."

She couldn't have said anything that would have made him feel worse. "Every family is different. We won't be together as much as some fathers and daughters are, but we'll still have each other."

None of them seemed to have much of an appetite after that, so they packed up the food and put the cooler back in Rosemary's car while Georgia and Bandit played in the grass. "This didn't go as well as I wanted it to," Abe said, choosing to downplay his real feelings about the picnic, that it was next door to a disaster.

They had to stop going on picnics.

"No, she needs more time. She's only three, and she doesn't understand everything yet."

Needs more time? He'd heard those words from Rosemary before.

He blew out a long breath between tight lips. Was she trying to say his relationship with Georgia wasn't going to work out either? Did she think he'd be a deadbeat dad?

Apparently so.

That's why it was up to him to prove her wrong.

He went to the truck to get the ball he'd brought along, and they started toward the cypress pond. On the way, they passed the stables and carriage house behind the mansion. Georgia breezed through both buildings, then they raced to the pond. She played with Bandit among the cypress knees for a while, and then they threw the ball together and played running games. Before long, Georgia began to lag behind them, eyes drooping.

Rosemary looked at her watch. "Time to go home for your nap."

Georgia trudged over to Abe and raised her arms. "Carry me, Daddy."

A new sensation hit him, something sweet and undefinable. His heart gave a thunderous lurch, the moment etching itself into his mind. Who knew the simple word held so much wonder? He savored the moment, sensing he'd never forget it.

He swept her off the ground, holding her in his arms.

She rubbed her eyes with her fists, seeming smaller than before, more vulnerable, counting on her daddy to take care of her.

And he would. Nothing would keep him from being a part of his daughter's life, from being a true father to her, despite the fact that Rosemary thought he wouldn't stick around. She'd soon see that his heart belonged to Georgia, and he would care for her as a father should.

Oh, yeah. He would definitely need to change Rosemary's mind.

Chapter Eight

Suddenly, everything seemed a little too perfect.

Abe came downstairs from his apartment above the gym Monday at midmorning, after lengthy phone conferences with both his accountant and his lawyer, and found Rosemary and Georgia in the Armstrong Kids room. While he'd been on the phone, everything had started falling into place there, even the delivery and installation of the playground equipment, which they could see through the glass side door. The new appliances had been installed, and apparently the bathroom had, too, since the fixtures that had arrived Saturday no longer sat in the main room. The kids' gym equipment had taken over one corner, and Rosemary unrolled a big rug off to one side.

Georgia pretended to cook in the little play kitchen, stirring something in a plastic pot and then giving her mother a taste. Seeing his daughter this morning, he knew he'd been right to call Joe Duncan and have him start a trust fund for Georgia and draw up a will, naming her Abe's heir. Even if he never got to live near her, he'd provide for her the best he could.

That way, Rosemary wouldn't have to work so hard either.

"I can't believe how much you got done this morning," he said, entering the cheery room.

Her tinkling laugh filled the air, making him smile. "All I did was boss around the plumber and the appliance delivery guy, arrange the toys and lay out this rug. But isn't it pretty?"

She pointed to the bright multicolored rug with an alphabet border and animal pictures to correspond with each letter.

"Everything in here looks pretty." Including Rosemary, looking sweet in her knee-length white running shorts and pink T-shirt, her hair in a high messy bun.

The sun shining through the door drew his attention, and he turned his focus there, since that was safer than thinking how cute his wife was. "Want to check out the playground with me, Georgia?"

She bounded over to him and grabbed his hand, chattering about swings and slides. Would he ever get used to the feel of her little fingers around his? He couldn't imagine this would ever get old.

He held the door, and they stepped into the fenced-in playground, complete with slides, tubes, climbers and swings. Georgia pulled away from him and ran to the nearest climber.

"Wait," Rosemary called, running toward her.

Too late. Just like that, the little girl was two feet off the ground, scaling that thing like a pro.

"She'll be all right," Abe said. "This equipment is designed for kids from two to twelve."

Rosemary blinked, her long lashes brushing her cheeks, and pulled Georgia from the climber. "Yes, but she's still very small."

Abe bit back the argument that wanted to force its way out. Kids needed to be kids. He took a deep breath, weighing his words. "Okay. Let's head inside and put the final touches on the kids' room. Are we on track for opening it tomorrow?"

"Sure. Everything's ready."

On the way in, his phone chimed out a boxing-bell notification. He read the text, then clicked on the phone number Lauren had added to her message. "Your new receptionist is doing a great job," he said to Rosemary, and he turned on the phone's speaker as he waited for his call to go through. "Colin called from the radio station."

When the news guy answered, he jumped right into his topic. "Abe, how about another interview at one? I've moved the schedule around to make it work."

He glanced at Rosemary, who smiled and nodded. "Sure. And don't worry. Rosemary can do the talking."

"Actually, I was hoping to get both her and the little girl."

Abe had seen that coming. "I'll check with her mom."

After promising Colin a quick callback, he pocketed his phone. "What do you think?"

She hesitated only a moment. "It's fine with me. The more exposure the gym gets, the better. Georgia, do you want to be on the radio again?"

She gave a few exaggerated nods, making her dark curls bounce.

"Let's announce the Armstrong Kids grand opening too," she said. "All I need to do is fill the refrigerator and cabinets with snacks and drinks."

Bandit started barking then, and Abe realized he hadn't taken the dog out for a while. "Georgia, want to help me walk the puppy?"

She ran over from the rug, where she'd been hopping from letter to letter and reciting the alphabet. "Where is he?"

"Upstairs, in my apartment."

"You live up there?" Georgia pointed to the steps.

He glanced at Rosemary, suddenly feeling awkward as he remembered his misgivings about raising a child above a gym. "I'll just go up and get him."

"I want to see your house," Georgia said.

Rosemary gave him a mischievous grin. "Or the three of us can go up together."

"That's your game, huh?" He smiled back, remembering how she used to make fun of what she called his micro-organized apartment back in the day. "I think you just want to check out my closet."

"Come on, Georgia. Let's beat him up the stairs!" Rosemary grabbed the little girl's hand and ran for the steps.

Abe followed, getting into the spirit of the game. "Faster, Georgia! You can beat your mama."

Upstairs, Georgia danced on the landing, celebrating. "I won!"

"You sure did." Abe pretended to huff and puff as he unlocked his apartment door and opened it for them.

They went in ahead of him and stopped just inside the living room. Rosemary turned slowly, taking it in, while the puppy jumped up on Georgia's legs. "Abe, this is amazing. It's so organized. Do you still hang your shirts according to color too?"

"How else can I find what I want? But before you sort the colors, you have to put the right kinds of shirts together. First come long-sleeve button-downs, then long-sleeve pullovers, then short-sleeve button-downs—"

"No, don't tell us!" Rosemary laughed and put her hands over her ears. "Don't listen, Georgia! You'll end up doing it too!"

Abe couldn't help laughing. "Then short-sleeve T-shirts, then gym shirts. Then you start with the colors. Black first, then blue, then brown—"

When Georgia and Rosemary started singing to cover up his voice, he opened the closet door. "See? It's not so bad."

Rosemary peered in while Georgia touched each shirt, naming the colors. "Are you kidding? Now your shoes are sorted by color too."

He looked at the shoe cubicles. Sure enough, they were.

Bandit's sudden outburst of whining reminded him they'd come up here to get the dog and take him outside to do his business. Not to look in his closets. "Georgia, his leash is hanging on the doorknob. Can you put it on him?"

She fumbled with it for a few moments, then Abe crouched down and helped her. He slipped the loop around her tiny wrist. "Hold tight, honey."

Downstairs, back in the gym, Mackenzie caught Rosemary's attention and waved her over. She turned the monitor for her to see, and the two immediately immersed themselves in whatever Mackenzie had on her mind.

Abe held the door for Georgia and Bandit, then he led them to the back of the lot where he'd been walking the pup. When Bandit had finished, they started back to the gym, Georgia chattering about dogs and little-girl interests Abe knew nothing about.

As they headed up the sidewalk to the front door, he saw movement from the corner of his eye.

A stray mixed-breed dog ran their way.

"Give me the leash, Georgia." He reached for it, but the bigger dog, smelling like it had just raided someone's garbage can, ran past them before Abe could slip the leash from the little girl's arm.

The dog was a blur by the time Abe realized Bandit was taking off after it. In a flurry of fur and the clamor of barks and yips, Georgia somehow ended up on all fours on the sidewalk, sending up a howl of her own, both knees skinned and bleeding.

He scooped her up in his arms, although she

clearly wasn't hurt badly. It was just a tumble and a few scrapes. But if he were to judge the severity of her injuries only by the racket she made, he'd call 911.

Rosemary met them at the entrance and opened the door, her mouth tight as she held out her hands. "Come here, baby."

Georgia's wails calmed to shuddering sobs. "No, I want Daddy."

What? Him?

The glow starting in his chest took a quick dousing when he caught the look in Rosemary's eyes—an agonizing mix of surprise and anguish—and her open mouth. "Uh, honey, maybe your mama should—"

"No." Rosemary closed her mouth and visibly swallowed, a fake smile twisting her lips. "You're her father. I'll go catch Bandit."

Right. In the clamor, he'd forgotten the pup. He watched her run after him and seize the leash, pick him up and cuddle him. She'd been great to take Georgia's words this way. As much as he loved hearing that his daughter wanted him, he didn't like to see Rosemary hurt.

With Georgia quieting even more, he started back to the entrance with her, Rosemary and Bandit close behind.

"So it's Daddy now, is it?"

He spun, recognizing the sharp voice.

No...

Sure enough, there stood Eldeen Rogers, her gossip antenna fully engaged. He remembered the first time Rosemary brought the judge to boxing class and Eldeen's snide remark about Georgia looking like Rosemary. How the woman had pretended to care about Abe's family, carrying over that gardenia plant his mom loved so much after his father left. Just so she could talk about them.

Of course she'd be the first person to learn he was Georgia's dad.

He'd been right about today. It was perfect.

A perfect crash and burn.

Leave it to Miss Eldeen to show up for the Natchez exposé of the decade.

Rosemary bit back the angry words she wanted to spout, remembering how Grannie had always shown mercy to this merciless woman, even when Miss Eldeen's gossip claws had sunk into their family. Rosemary gave her the most authentic smile she could muster. "I'm surprised to see you here, since it's not a boxing-class day. Can we help you with something?"

Then she noticed the older woman had on high-end athleisure pants and shirt, her bottle-black hair pulled back in a perfect bun. Not messy like Rosemary's.

"I'm meeting your grandmother in ten minutes. So let's get me registered for a membership right away. We're going to walk on the treadmill while we discuss the pageant."

"Sure." Rosemary held the door as Miss Eldeen sailed into the gym with as much attitude as she'd had back when the Natchez Historical Society named her Benefactress of the Year. Since the pageant was her favorite topic, maybe Rosemary could divert her attention away from her and Abe and onto the upcoming performance. "I hope nothing has gone wrong with the pageant. You usually have everything lined out long before now."

Miss Eldeen leaned closer. "There's been quite a scandal." She lowered her voice to a whisper. "Anna Mathilda Conner was to be in the children's sketch, but her parents have separated. This morning she and her mother moved to Mobile, poor things, so we need to select another girl."

Rosemary had known Miss Eldeen long enough to know she sympathized with Anna Mathilda because she had to move away from Natchez, not because her family had broken up. "You shouldn't have any trouble finding a replacement. Every Natchez girl under the age of six would love to take her spot."

"Yes, well. You know it's not as simple as that."

Rosemary took the clipboard with a membership form attached from Lauren. She handed it to Miss Eldeen along with a pen. "Why not?"

Her gaze sharpened. "You've been away too long. You've forgotten that we like the pageant performers to be related to former participants. Preferably kings and queens. The tourists expect it. And they'll descend on Natchez in less than a week for the spring festival."

"I'm sure you and Grannie will figure something out." Rosemary glanced over at the Armstrong Kids room, where Abe had sat Georgia on the counter and now cleaned her knees, the first-aid kit beside her. When he bent over and gently kissed both of her scrapes, Rosemary's eyes filled. What was it about a big, strong man showing tenderness to a child? And when he stood again, their daughter stretched her arms to wrap them around his neck.

Oh, my heart...

Rosemary ran her fingers under her eyes, swiping away her tears before Miss Eldeen could notice. But seeing Abe and Georgia, acting for all the world like the father and daughter they were, Rosemary knew she had to make a decision.

It was a given that Miss Eldeen would spread the word of Georgia's paternity before the day was out. So should Rosemary continue to keep their marriage a secret from everyone? Or should she admit they were married, which also meant admitting her husband had left her after two weeks of marriage?

Even though she was twenty-three years old, she still had to consider her father. He'd said he'd quit his boxing class if she "got close" to Abe again. Which would mean he'd go backward in his newfound improvements, however small, and miss out on further progress. There were also his threats against Abe's family. When he'd said he'd go after the entire Armstrong family if she didn't stay away from him, he'd meant it. And he had the power to do it. Would he follow through now, knowing Abe was Georgia's father?

All paid up and signed in, Miss Eldeen sat in the foyer chair facing the desk, as if she meant to keep an eye on Rosemary.

Fine. She could watch her all she wanted. Rosemary whipped her phone from her pocket and opened her to-do list app.

Check with Lauren about new memberships and class sign-ups.

Right.

Minutes later, as Mackenzie reported the eighteen new memberships and three new classes over the weekend, Grannie pulled up in her myrtle-bedecked golf cart.

Just the person she needed to talk to.

She excused herself from Mackenzie and ambled toward the door, trying not to alert Miss Eldeen of Grannie's presence, although Rosemary wanted to sprint to her grandmother's side. In the parking lot, she clasped Grannie's arm.

"I need to talk to you. In private." She glanced around, searching for a place to hide from Miss Eldeen's all-seeing eyes. "The playground."

"We have a playground now?" Grannie took her time putting her cart in neutral, setting the brake, turning it off and pocketing the key.

"Hurry. Miss Eldeen's already here. She might see us."

Grannie visibly shifted into business mode, and they hurried to sit together on the swings. When Rosemary had told her what happened, Grannie paused, her lips pursed as she assumed her thinking pose. "So Abe is Georgia's father. I suspected it all along. But why didn't you tell me?"

"You know Daddy. She's going to blab this all over town," Rosemary said.

"And she'll embellish the story like a garden club queen's crown." Grannie shook her head. "She's the one who used to write the gossip column in the *Natchez Courier*. When they quit running that column back in the nineties, she and her cronies started forwarding gossipy emails to each other. Now they use social media."

Rosemary let out a groan. "I can't even refute anything she'll say. I closed all my social media accounts."

"Then scoop the story."

Scoop? "What do you mean?"

"Find a way to make it public. Be the one to tell Natchez who Georgia's father is. Everybody who knew you two then has probably figured it out anyway. Then it'll be old news, and no one will pay any attention to Eldeen."

Rosemary could do it on the afternoon radio broadcast.

But there was the other issue…

Lord, should I tell Grannie my biggest secret? Please show me what to do.

She drew a deep breath, listening with her heart.

With a growing sense of peace, she breathed another quick prayer for the right words. She pulled her locket from beneath her shirt and held it out for Grannie to see. "There's something else you don't know. Remember my eighteenth birthday, when you took me to your room and gave me your mother's silver locket?"

"Yes, and I asked you to wear it at your wedding, as my mother and I did."

Rosemary pushed herself out of the swing and stood in front of her grandmother. "Grannie," she whispered, "that's exactly what I did."

Grannie blinked, her mouth hanging open. "You mean…"

"Nobody else knows this, but Abe and I got married two weeks before he left for the army, and we're still married."

After a span of seconds that felt like an hour, her grandmother closed her mouth, stood and crossed her arms in front of her. "If I can't discern enough to realize my own granddaughter has gotten married, then I need to turn in my matchmaker license."

"We've kept it a secret all this time."

Her grandmother's eyes grew wide. "Why?"

"Because of Daddy. Do you remember what happened to Cody Lewis's family?"

"Didn't they leave town shortly after the kerfuffle at your party?"

"Yes, but not voluntarily. Daddy called in a favor at the cannery and had his father transferred. He threatened to keep Miss Anise from getting a job at the hospital if Abe and I didn't stop seeing each other."

"I need to sit down." Grannie sat back in the swing. Then she lowered her voice so Rosemary had to strain to hear her. "You never moved out…"

Rosemary slumped in the swing. "I was a pathetic wife. Abe begged me to move into his apartment with him, but I knew what my father was capable of. When Abe gave me an ultimatum, I chickened out, and he left."

A cool breeze whispered across her forehead, bringing a little comfort. "I guess he thought there was no use in being married if your wife won't live with you."

"Rosemary, you don't have to go back to the island."

What? Of course she did.

"You can stay here and get to know Abe again. Let him get to know Georgia more. I never could figure out what happened between you. Everyone used to say what a perfect match you were. I still believe it."

"No, it's too late."

"There's not a speck of truth in that."

How Rosemary wished her grandmother was right. But she hadn't been there that night, hadn't heard the pain and anger in Abe's voice.

"All my life," Grannie said, "I've stood on one Bible verse, John 11:25—'I am the resurrection, and the life. He that believeth in me, though he were dead, yet shall he live.'"

Rosemary nodded. "When Jesus raised Lazarus from the dead."

"Right. Lazarus had been dead three days. That means he was beyond dead—he had begun to decompose and he stunk. But Jesus didn't say it was too late. He told the dead man's sisters that he would live again. And he did. Because Jesus resurrected him."

If only Grannie was right and she and Abe could go back to the way things were before his impossible ultimatum. Back when they always told each other their sorrows and then just sat and held each other, so nothing could hurt them.

But this marriage had been dead a lot longer than three days.

"Lazarus could have been dead four years, and Jesus still could have raised him from the dead. He can raise your marriage too."

Now that would take an intervention from God.

She decided to change the subject, since this one was making her sadder by the second. "I think you're right, and I should reveal Abe as Georgia's father before Eldeen can do it. But what about the marriage?"

"What good would it do to tell the world about that?" Grannie said in her no-nonsense manner. "All it would do is relieve you from feeling guilty about something you didn't do. Eldeen will run you down to her gossipy friends, but who listens to her, other than a few women whose opinions shouldn't matter to you?"

Rosemary gave her grandmother a quick hug. "Thank you, Grannie. You always know what to do."

"You'll know, too, when the time comes." Grannie started for the door. "I have to go. Besides the pageant problem, I have a dilemma of my own. Right now I'm trying to find a widower as a match for Eldeen. Believe me, I don't know what to do about that."

Why were relationships so complex?

Rosemary looked at her watch. Quarter till twelve. In an hour and fifteen minutes, she'd scoop Miss Eldeen. And enjoy it.

Chapter Nine

"It's all over." Rance Bailey flopped into the chair on the other side of Abe's desk, his ever-present grin missing from his pudgy face. "I'm closing the coffee shop before the bank can fore-close."

He had to be kidding.

But one look at Rance's droopy eyes and Abe knew his next-door merchant friend, about ten years older than Abe, was serious. "I knew busi-ness was slow, but do you have to shutter the shop?"

"I have to face facts. The shop wasn't doing well even before the cannery shut down on the next block. I lost all that morning business, which was keeping me going."

"Can't you do anything to stay afloat? Get a loan?"

Even as he said it, Abe knew he'd make the

same choice in that position. One thing he'd learned from his father's many mistakes: don't take on debt.

"I've already borrowed to the limit. Every time I see JD in church or on the street, I'm afraid he's going to call my loans. It's time to try something different."

Abe thought about offering to get Rance a cup of coffee but then figured it might make him feel even worse. He reached into his dorm fridge beside his desk and pulled out a water bottle instead and gave it to him. "What can I do to help?"

Rance twisted off the lid and took a long swig. "Rent's due day after tomorrow, so I'm closing today and clearing out everything. I want to try to sell some of the fixtures and supplies to get cash so I can start fresh. I was wondering if you still have empty space in the gym."

"Not as much as I did, since we made the showroom into the kids' room. But yeah, I have some space in the back. You want to store some stuff?"

"I'd appreciate it. I can pay a little for storage."

Abe waved away the offer. "What are you going to do?"

His grin looked a little forced. "Head to Jackson. There's this girl there…"

Rance Bailey with a girl? Now this was news. "Who is she?"

"Her name is Kimmy. I wouldn't admit this to anyone else, but yeah, she's sort of bailing me out of this mess. When Miss—when I met her, I told her everything, how my business was failing and I was in debt up to my neck, but she says she loves me." His pale blue eyes turned soft looking. "Kimmy wants to help me get back on my feet. She's a good woman."

Wow, that must have been humbling for him to admit. But wasn't Rosemary doing the same thing, in a way, for Abe? He'd never expected her to put in as many hours and work as hard as she did. Especially since she took care of her parents and that big old house of theirs in the evenings.

The similarity surprised him, until he started to wonder how much alike he and Rance really were. They each had a good woman giving herself for them, and they each had a business that wasn't making ends meet...

Rance's shop sat right next door, in the same building as the gym. Sure, they'd had six more new memberships today and a lot more traffic. But if Natchez Coffee Shop could fail, the gym could too.

"What's happening next for you?" Abe asked, half afraid to hear the answer.

"Some of the guys from church are going to help me move my stuff tonight. I've already cleared out my apartment. On Wednesday, I'm driving to Jackson, and on Friday, we're getting married. We want to start up a little shop there, but this time, Kimmy is going to be the manager."

At least Rance was smart enough to let her do it.

When he left, Abe pulled up his accounting software and took a hard look at his financials. His books were probably in better shape than Rance's, but the gym still wasn't making enough. The first financial emergency would make him dip into the rest of his inheritance, and he needed to keep that buffer. And now he needed to start giving money to Rosemary every month to help with Georgia.

Suddenly this felt a little like the summer his dad took off with a strange woman and left behind a foreclosure notice and heavy credit card and loan debt. Which his mom had just recently finished paying.

A small part of him envied Rance and his ability to take off and start over in a new place. But it wouldn't work for Abe. Not after all he'd gone through when his father pulled the same stunt.

No, Abe would break the chain of irresponsibility, of unfaithfulness in his family. And he'd make sure he kept the gym running. For his family's sake and for Pastor David's sake. Rock Steady Boxing would continue, and he'd support his daughter and help Rosemary too. He didn't yet know how, but he'd do it.

No matter what it took.

For once, Rosemary was thankful for Grannie's golf cart.

From the day that cart was delivered, Rosemary had been convinced her grandmother would somehow get hurt, driving it wherever she wanted to go in Natchez. But today, after she and Miss Eldeen had finished their workout, Grannie had loaded her garden club friend into the little electric cart and whisked her away for a late lunch. And, no doubt, to stall her gossiping.

At Abe's desk with him and Georgia, Rosemary answered the call from Colin and hit the speaker button while Abe checked his email. Grandmother had been right. After he'd introduced Rosemary, she knew what to do. "All three of us are here at Armstrong Gym today— me, Georgia and her daddy, Abe."

She glanced at Georgia. As she'd expected, their daughter hadn't raised her head from the picture she was drawing.

Abe looked up slowly from his laptop screen.

He caught and held her gaze as if he wanted to jump up and catch her in his arms.

"Rosemary..." His hoarse whisper, little more than a breath, dropped upon her heart and warmed it somehow.

As Colin's voice brought her back to the moment, asking about tomorrow's opening of Armstrong Kids, Abe's phone vibrated. He picked it up, glanced at it and stepped out of the office. Moments later, her own phone buzzed.

When the interview ended, she checked her messages and found a text from Abe.

Pastor David fell. Be back later.

Georgia had fallen asleep on Abe's office floor, so Rosemary hurried to the Armstrong Kids room and put away the snacks and paper products she'd bought over lunch hour. During the radio interview, she'd promised to open the childcare at seven in the morning, so she had to be ready. She instructed Mackenzie to edit the website to reflect the changes, including the addition of three new exercise classes.

While running the vacuum, Rosemary made a mental list of her tasks for the evening: pick up Daddy at the courthouse, bake pork chops and make scalloped potatoes and salad for supper, and thaw a roast for tomorrow night. As she searched her mind, trying to remember if she needed to do anything else, Lauren came into the kids' room. Rosemary turned off the vacuum.

"Abe took Pastor David to the ER. He won't be back before we close," Lauren said.

Two hours later, Rosemary was taking the pork chops out of the oven when her phone rang. She pulled it from her back pocket. Abe.

"Pastor David's okay but shook up. He fell in the yard and had pain in his hip, so we got it x-rayed. He has some bad bruises and a couple of scrapes, but no broken bones."

"That's good news." She glanced at the pan of meat. "I have extra chops. Tell him I'll bring them over for his supper. If he feels up to it, I'll pack enough for all four of us."

"Hang on, and I'll check." After a moment, he came back. "He said he'd enjoy the company."

After they hung up, she grabbed a casserole dish from the cabinet and loaded it with pork chops and potatoes. Then she headed for the sitting room, where Daddy sat at his desk as usual before supper. Georgia played with her dolls on the floor in front of Mama's recliner.

As Rosemary knelt down on the floor and wrapped Georgia in a hug, her daughter looked up at her with the sweetest smile ever, her love glowing in her eyes. It soothed the sting of knowing all her friends here would view Rosemary differently now, since they were smart enough to figure out that Abe had abandoned her. She touched her silver locket. Yes, this little girl was worth all the awkwardness and hardship that had come with her unusual arrival into the world.

Rosemary turned to her own mother, who was fluffing the quilt that lay in the doll cradle. "Mama, Pastor David's on his way home from the ER. I thought I'd take him some supper."

"Good idea. Send along a couple pieces of the Lady Baltimore cake Miss Eldeen brought over this afternoon too."

Daddy swiveled slowly in his chair and looked at her with clearer eyes than she'd seen for a while. "Olivia had the radio playing in the office this afternoon while I was in court, and she heard you on the radio."

Not good. Rosemary got up and sat on the sofa, waiting for the outburst to come.

"I warned you not to get close to him, and you knew I didn't want all of Natchez to know he was Georgia's father."

"We're not close." Well, not in the way her father meant. They were friends now, but not close—not romantically. Although she couldn't deny that she'd been remembering a lot of reasons she'd fallen in love with him. "And everybody probably figured it out anyway. The whole town knows I never dated."

"Never dated anyone except Abe."

Was he remembering the same childhood she was? "No, I never dated anybody, at least, not real dates, like a movie or going out for a burger like the rest of the kids. Other than sneaking around at picnic spots and eating at a restaurant together in New Orleans, Abe and I never dated. Because you wouldn't let me."

"Actions have consequences. After this humiliation, I don't want to go back to that boxing class and look at Abe Armstrong twice a week. So I'm quitting."

He had to be kidding.

Mama put down the baby doll Georgia had given her to dress. "No, you're not, Burley. You're going right back to that gym tomorrow to take your class."

"You've made progress from just two classes, Daddy. You have to keep going."

"I don't know why you keep saying that, because it's not true." He turned back to the ledger he was working in, but he didn't pick up his pen. Instead, he merely sat there alone on the far side of the room. "I've made my decision. I'm not going back."

"I've made my decision too," Rosemary said, careful to keep her tone respectful. "Part of the reason I came here was to be your corner person, since Mama couldn't. I'll be at your office at nine thirty tomorrow morning to take you to boxing class."

When she got no response other than a snort from her father, Rosemary stood and started for the kitchen. "I need to get to Pastor David's house. He should be home by now."

She left the room, her father's words still burning in her mind. What was he thinking? Did he want to hurt Abe by quitting his boxing class? Of course it would, the way he poured himself into each boxer. But he'd also feel a measure of relief.

Maybe all this was her fault. She'd known she might regret her decision to make Abe and Georgia's relationship public like that. And if Daddy continued to decline, or if he fell again…

Reaching the kitchen, she found Grannie Eugenia rummaging through the refrigerator.

"I did as you suggested," Rosemary said, grabbing plastic containers to hold salad and cake. "I got on the radio and told the whole town that Abe is Georgia's father."

"I heard it. Eldeen and I, and the rest of the garden club, had a late lunch at the Carriage House. They had the radio on." Grannie pulled her head out of the refrigerator and held out a mason jar full of kimchi. "I had called in a few favors, and we voted to ask Georgia to fill in for Anna Mathilda in the children's skit at the pageant."

Rosemary took the jar from her. Was she going to put that stuff on her pork chop? At least Rosemary wouldn't be here to smell it. "Georgia will be excited. Did you tell her?"

"Not without asking you first."

"It's fine." She set the jar on the table and pulled the salad from the fridge.

When she started packing the food into a basket, Grannie handed her the kimchi again. "This is for Pastor David. I made it myself. Take Georgia with you tonight. Rehearsal starts at six thirty."

"Right."

"And, Rosemary? I heard what your daddy said." Grannie drew near and gave her a rare, quick hug. "You made the best choice."

She could only hope her grandmother was right.

Chapter Ten

As Abe helped Rosemary set the table in Pastor David's kitchen, he could hardly keep his mind off the words she'd spoken for all of Natchez to hear.

All three of us are here at Armstrong Gym today—me, Georgia and her daddy, Abe.

Of course, she hadn't decided to tell the world he was Georgia's father because she'd suddenly stopped being ashamed of him. If she hadn't revealed that secret, Miss Eldeen would have, and they both knew it. Still, the announcement had changed everything between them, and between him and his town. With Rosemary, hopefully for the better. With Natchez citizens, probably for the worse. Because who can respect a man who'd abandoned the mother of his unborn child?

"Pastor David must think a lot of you, since

you're the one he called when he needed help," Rosemary said, placing forks beside their plates and wearing a blue dress that matched her eyes.

"I owe him a lot. And I don't mean just the tuition he paid for Jase and me or all the food he and Miss Pauline brought over when we were kids. And everything else they did." He opened the refrigerator door and took out cans of ginger ale. "He keeps these here for me when I come over. Do you let Georgia have soft drinks?"

"On special occasions. I'll share one with her tonight. She'll like that." She reached for glasses from the cabinet. "The garden club has asked Georgia to be in the children's skit at the pageant, and she has her first practice tonight. I thought you might like to go."

After what she'd revealed this morning on the radio, this was a brave step for Rosemary. "The judge will find out if we go together."

She winced a little. "The judge has already given me his verdict. Because I made the radio announcement, he's not coming to boxing class tomorrow. At least that's what he said. I think I'll be able to change his mind in the morning, even if I have to guilt him into doing it."

"Guilt isn't always bad."

The meal ready, Abe set down the cans and started for the living room, where Georgia entertained Pastor David with her antics and chattering.

"Ask my daddy, and he'll teach you how not to fall down again so you don't get hurt," she said, her heart in her eyes. His sweet, loving little girl—just like her mama.

"We need to talk about the bomb Rosemary dropped on the radio," the pastor said after Georgia skipped into the kitchen. He grabbed his cane and got up from his recliner while Abe spotted him.

"How'd you know about that? You were on the ground in the yard during the broadcast." Abe grabbed the ice pack the pastor had been using on his hip, and they took their time moving toward the kitchen.

"Your mama told me in the ER. They had the radio on."

The wave of embarrassment washing over Abe must have shown on his face, because Pastor David gave him a fatherly shoulder punch. He hadn't thought about the fact that his mother would have to live this down too. He pictured her in an ER exam room, trying to save some patient's life while the nurses whispered about her son.

He was starting to hate secrets.

"What happened between you and Rosemary is in the past. We all stumble in different areas.

The important thing is to move on without continuing to make the same wrong decisions."

Well, he was right about that. And about the fact that Abe had handled the whole situation wrong back then. He'd been wrong to leave, to refuse to listen to Rosemary.

To give in to his pride.

Abe kept his hand on Pastor David's upper arm, ready to help in case he stumbled as he lowered himself to the colonial armchair at the kitchen table. He placed the ice pack at his hip and took his place across the table from Rosemary, where he had a clear view of her beautiful blue eyes, which spoke only kindness, gentleness to him. Despite the trouble his leaving had caused.

But Abe was no longer the same person he'd been back then. And now that their secret was out—at least, one of their secrets—he intended to prove it.

Later, in the City Auditorium two blocks from the river, Abe had the distinct feeling every parent, grandparent and garden club member in the pull-down seats was staring at him. Whispering about him.

But when Georgia danced with the other little kids, each holding a different-colored shiny ribbon, he suddenly didn't care. The little ham smiled and waved at the small audience the entire time, drawing chuckles from even Miss Eldeen.

Rosemary's grandmother slid into the seat beside her and raised her phone, taking a picture of the kids. "Tourists are already trickling into town."

"It's started," he said, grinning. The spring festival wouldn't affect his gym, but it always boosted tourism.

"Both your mothers are taking their turns giving tours of the town. I chose to be a tour guide at a couple of the museums this year. We never have enough volunteers for the festival." She gave Rosemary a sidewise glance, then resumed her picture taking. "If you could stay longer, you could help too."

"Stay?" Rosemary said as if she'd never heard the word before. He couldn't quite place the expression in her eyes. Sadness? Longing?

Miss Eugenia snapped a picture of her. "Think about it. But for now, could you and Abe go outside and pose for a picture? They want some shots of former kings and queens, and you're the only couple here tonight."

"No." Apparently, Rosemary had caught her slightest emphasis on the word *couple*, judging from her quick response. "I'll have to take Georgia home as soon as the children's skit is over."

"Didn't you read the itinerary? We're going

over the first fifteen minutes of the show twice tonight." Her grandmother held out a photocopy of a handwritten paper. "We'll be here another half hour, at the least. Why don't you take a few pictures and then run to the seamstress for me and pick up our gowns? I walked here tonight instead of driving my golf cart, so I can't."

"What about Georgia?"

"Don't worry about Georgia, because I'll be right here. In fact, I'll walk home with her."

"Does it have to be tonight? The seamstress is way across town."

"It's a full three-minute drive in my golf cart." Miss Eugenia gave her that tight-lipped smile she always used when she wanted her way. "Yes, it has to be tonight. We can't wait until the last minute, in case the alterations need more adjustment."

Rosemary turned to Abe, an apology in her gaze. "Is that okay with you?"

He nodded, noting the gleam in Miss Eugenia's eye. Did she like winning a disagreement that much?

As they started for the steps to the entrance, he turned around to catch one more glimpse of his daughter beside the maypole. He might be fooling himself, but she had to be the prettiest girl in the room. Other than her mother.

Her great-grandmother must have thought so,

too, as many pictures as she had taken while they'd been sitting together. But now, as he watched her, she wasn't taking pictures. Instead, she looked like she was texting. Then she spun around as if she'd sensed him watching her. Miss Eugenia caught his eye and hurried off in the other direction, cramming the phone into her little purse as if she was afraid Abe might see what she'd texted.

She'd been on the eccentric side as long as he'd known her, which was all his life, so he let her go and caught up to Rosemary halfway up the steps.

Outside, Cassius Cole, the balding *Natchez Courier* reporter and photographer with a huge camera on a strap around his neck, stood pecking at his oversize phone. Seeing Abe and Rosemary, he shoved the phone into his slacks pocket, looking as guilty as Miss Eugenia had.

What was wrong with people tonight?

"Are you okay with us taking a picture together?" he whispered to Rosemary.

She nodded. "It's okay."

"You look even better than you did the year you were queen," Cassius said in his old-Natchez accent. About the same age as Miss Eugenia, Cassius probably needed a human-interest story to help keep his great-grandfather's newspaper alive in the digital age. "I didn't remember you being a king, Abe."

He drew a breath, then let it out in a little growl. "I wasn't really. The club's first choice, Willard Leech, got appendicitis the afternoon of the first show, and I was the only other eligible guy in town who fit the costume."

"Ah, yes. I'd forgotten about poor Willard. Because of that incident, they try to choose smaller men now." He lifted his camera and pointed it in the direction of the closer of the front lawn's two giant live oaks. "Let's take a picture under that one."

A few girls from their high school class had gathered under the tree, apparently to give advice on their poses, hair and whatever else they could find to fix. When they'd convinced Rosemary to take down her hair and put on some lipstick, she and Abe stood a few inches apart and endured a barrage of shots from both Cassius and the women.

"I think that's enough," Rosemary said, her dark curls blowing a little in the breeze.

"The kings always try to get a kiss after the crowning," one of the girls said. Was her name Kayla? Kylie? He couldn't remember, but he didn't miss the sarcasm in her tone. "Maybe you need to be the one to try now, Rosemary."

The smirks on the other women's faces made

Abe want to walk away. But the embarrassment in Rosemary's sweet eyes set a fire inside him.

Sure, he'd been a jerk back then, thinking only of his own pain and not appreciating her. But this was Rosemary they were taunting, the woman who'd helped him through his hardest times, back when his dad left, and made him see there was more to life than making ends meet. Who'd believed in him when nearly everybody thought he was nobody—just the boy whose dad had made a fool of his family.

She'd given him hope.

Still gave him hope.

All they knew was that he'd left her, a pregnant nineteen-year-old, when he joined the army. Did they think he'd refuse to stand up for her now?

If so, they were wrong.

"No, she doesn't have to try to get a kiss from me." He drew closer, took her in his arms, lowered his voice to a whisper. "Kiss me as if it were the—" he stopped, searched his mind, his heart, and tailored the famous line "—first time."

Her eyes grew wide, then slid shut as she moved almost imperceptibly nearer, and he kissed her.

She smelled of orange blossom and tasted of

sweet ginger, and as he entwined his fingers in her tangle of hair, he pulled her closer yet.

And as she kissed him back, he felt a gradual tugging in his heart, an undefinable sweetness that took his breath. Beautiful, kind, gentle Rosemary, in his arms again…

The flash of a camera reminded him they were not alone.

Rosemary jerked from his arms so fast he wobbled a little from the force of it. He found his balance and turned toward the flash, catching a little gasp from Rosemary.

"Really?" Her voice shook. "You took a picture of that?" She spun away from the photographer and strode off, heading down the sidewalk.

Abe turned on the photographer. "Cassius, don't you have any sense?"

"It was a great moment. What chemistry! It'll look fantastic in the *Courier*'s special festival edition. Maybe even in next year's pageant program."

"No. You are not printing that picture," he yelled as he sprinted after Rosemary. Then he realized where she was going.

To the river.

To the gazebo.

He slowed to a stop. Should he follow? Jase had told him the story of how she'd run to the gazebo the night he left. How he'd seen her the next morning during his daily run, huddled against the railing in the damp river air, in her safe place.

Maybe she'd rather be alone.

Then again, leaving her alone hadn't exactly been the smartest move last time. If nothing else, he owed her an apology for the way this kiss fiasco had turned out.

Although the kiss itself—wow. As much as he wanted to completely regret that, he couldn't. Even though he knew how much trouble it would cause between them...

He started down the street again at a slower pace, giving her time. But not too much time.

At the end of the block, he made a left onto Broadway and headed south. Finally, he caught a glimpse of her blue dress. In the distance, she stood on the pedestrian bridge over Roth Hill Road, facing the river.

Interesting that she'd stopped before reaching the gazebo, the total opposite of what he'd expected. What made her go to the bridge instead? One thing Abe knew: he wasn't leaving her until he found out.

The sun had started to sink behind the Natchez-Vidalia Bridge and turn the sky and river into an amazing blazing red, more spectacular than any sunset Rosemary had ever seen on the island.

And how appropriate was it, following that epic kiss? Wow, Abe had not forgotten how to kiss during the years they'd been apart.

She needed to forget that kiss, although it would be hard to do.

And naturally he'd fractured the classic *Casablanca* line. But what exactly had he said? She searched her mind for a moment, then his words came crashing back.

Kiss me as if it were the first time...

Of course, Ilsa, not Rick, had said that line in *Casablanca*. But Ilsa had told Rick to kiss her as if it were the last time, not the first.

Just before she left him.

What had Abe meant? Was he merely being silly, trying to make her laugh, as usual?

That couldn't be it. What man tried to make a woman laugh when he was about to kiss her the way Abe had kissed Rosemary? Did he mean to tell her he was taking off again? Surely he wouldn't leave his family and his business, even his ministry as Rock Steady Boxing coach— and Georgia—just to get away from Rosemary. Or would history repeat itself? He'd left her, his family and his landscaping business once before...

She stopped the thought cold. No, if he intended to leave her, he would have told her to kiss him like the last time, as Ilsa had. And besides, she was the one who'd run from him just now, not the other way around.

To her amazement, she realized Abe did seem to be changing. And she had to admit, if only to herself, that her feelings toward him had been swelling like the flooded Mississippi.

As for the rest of the encounter, she could excuse Cassius, since he wasn't exactly known for tact or discernment. The mean girls from school were another story altogether. A part of her wished she'd had a wedding ring to flash before their mocking eyes.

But even that wouldn't have accomplished anything. They still would have been right that Abe had left her. And she could do nothing to soften that harsh reality.

She'd turned at Roth Hill Road, a street leading to the riverbank, the first spot on the north end of Broadway to reveal the entire width of the river. It was a relief to get off the sidewalk and onto the small Roth Hill footbridge.

As she stopped for a moment to watch the river from this vantage, her tense muscles started to relax. No big surprise that she felt less sheltered here, more vulnerable, than she'd feel at the gazebo. Nonetheless, the sight of the

Mississippi calmed her as always, its current rolling and its waters moving, always moving.

"And of his fulness have all we received, and grace for grace."

The verse from John's gospel flowed through her mind. Just as the mighty Mississippi continually flowed by, giving water for water and never stopping, grace also tumbled through and never stopped, always supplying, never depleting. When one form of grace had done its job, another came to take its place.

No matter what Abe did or what Daddy did, grace would be here. Never abandoning her, never manipulating her.

Grace was here.

Grace would always be here.

Chapter Eleven

Abe's first glimpse of Rosemary's face twisted his gut and brought a fresh sense of pain, of shame. She'd walked away from Cassius with so much dignity and control he'd have thought the whole mess had meant nothing to her. But now, catching her with her guard down, he saw the truth. Between the photographer's tasteless actions and their old classmates' catty words, Rosemary had been hurt.

Deeply hurt.

But by whom? Cassius and the girls—or him?

He picked up his pace, calling her name as he approached.

She lifted her gaze, met his, dropped it.

When he reached her side, she turned and leaned on the bridge's railing, looking out toward the river. "You knew where to find me."

Of course he did. At least, he'd known the

general vicinity. "I thought you'd go to the gazebo."

"So did I. This view of the river drew me, though. I haven't often watched it from here."

He hesitated, unsure what to say. "The river has drawn you as long as I can remember."

"Mama says I got it from her third-great-grandmother, Clarissa Montgomery. Clarissa used to spend a lot of time on the river, ministering to the poor."

"In Natchez Under the Hill?"

She nodded. "You know how rough Under the Hill was back in the day. Clarissa's father built a mission hotel there as a safe place for women and families to stay when they got off the boats. Apparently the river meant something to her too."

"Yeah, maybe." He sidled up to the fence, rested his arms on it and looked out at the water, waiting for her to say more. She surely had more on her mind than nostalgia over a long-gone relative who'd died maybe two centuries before Rosemary was born.

But she had a habit of silence at times, like now. She didn't talk a man's head off but spoke only when she had something of value to say. She rarely got involved in foolish chatter, and never the way those girls had at the photoshoot.

He hadn't realized it before, but that was part of the reason he'd fallen for her.

Not that she didn't talk, because she did. But she always made him feel at ease. Like she was now. Even after the embarrassing event they'd just gone through, she didn't complain or gripe about it. She'd merely told a little story about a forgotten woman who'd somehow influenced her life through the generations.

He cleared his throat, unsure how to bring up the subject they were avoiding. "I was thinking maybe we should talk about…you know…"

"The kiss."

"Yeah." Her tone felt a little too matter-of-fact to him. Which probably indicated the topic meant more to her than she let on.

"I don't even know how all that happened," she said. "We went out there for a picture, that's all."

"Those girls were always jealous of you." Abe kept his focus on the water and the sky as they turned a deeper red by the minute. "They couldn't stand the fact that you were the sweetest and most beautiful girl in school. Tonight they had an opportunity to embarrass you, and they did. And I'm sorry."

She turned to him, her brow furrowed. "They were jealous because they all wanted to go out with you."

"Me?" Abe's voice rose an octave. "No girls wanted to go out with me. I was a nobody."

"You were not. You certainly aren't now."

He shook his head. "I never could understand why you had anything to do with me. You had it all. You were smart, pretty, nice to everyone. And you had a family. A home. I had nothing to offer you."

Oh, but there was a lot more to it than that. She'd been compassionate and generous and had about a hundred other qualities that had made him fall for her, hard.

The worst part was that he'd begun to see those things again, to remember why he used to want to spend every moment with her.

But that was a dangerous thought to dwell on.

"Abe, there's one more thing." Her sweet eyes turned sad, as if she'd rather jump into the river than say what she had to say. "You don't ever have to—don't feel obligated to—"

In an instant, he understood, and it felt like a punch to his throat. "Kiss you again."

"I know why you did it. You wanted to protect my feelings after those girls insulted me, to keep me from feeling like a castoff in front of them. I get it. And I appreciate it. But don't feel like you have to do that for me again."

Apparently it hadn't affected her as much as it had affected him. Because now that his anger at Cassius and the girls had pretty much died down, he admitted the kiss had been special. Bonding. Life changing. For him at least. It had helped him realize he did have feelings for Rosemary. Whether they were old feelings stirred up by the kiss or new feelings inspired by it, he didn't know. Might never know.

But clearly it hadn't meant the same to her.

He'd need to guard his heart better. Keep a distance, if that were possible when they spent all day together every day and shared a daughter.

But he'd do it. He wouldn't let these feelings blossom into love. Apparently she still intended to leave in a week and return to island life.

Which was fine with him. Because it kind of had to be.

At some point in the night, Rosemary decided to stop using all her emotional energy thinking about the kiss—that perfect kiss. Since sleep wouldn't come anyway, she got up and checked on Georgia in the next room, then powered up her laptop. This afternoon, Abe had emailed her his financial reports from the past four weeks. She found the document, opened it and read the whole thing again.

They were missing something.

Rosemary didn't know what it was. But

they'd missed some big income opportunity for the gym.

She'd tried to figure it out earlier, after she and Abe walked back to his truck, they'd picked up the alterations for Grannie, and he'd dropped her off at Pastor David's house to get her car. Memberships and traffic were up but not enough. In fact, even Colin was there. They'd started three women's exercise classes and three senior classes, thanks to Grannie's and Miss Eldeen's input and influence. The weight room usually had at least ten or twelve members working out during prime times, and she'd counted twenty-two later in the day yesterday, after most people got off work. The daycare would open in the morning, and she'd announced kids' after-school and upcoming summer events on the radio that afternoon.

So what were they missing?

Realizing she was not going to fall asleep anytime soon, Rosemary closed the computer and grabbed her robe at the foot of the bed. Maybe a warm drink would help her sleep.

Downstairs in the kitchen, she reached for a mug, filled it with milk and put it in the microwave. Just as she'd taken it out and sweetened it with a spoonful of sugar, she heard the door creak open and shut to Grannie's wing.

"You can't sleep either?" Grannie asked, tying the sash on her robe.

"Too much on my mind."

"Me too. What are you drinking?"

"Warm milk."

"Good idea. I'll join you."

But instead of pouring milk into her mug, Grannie filled it with blueberry kefir and put it in the microwave for a few seconds. "You don't ever want to heat kefir too long. It'll kill the good bacteria."

Rosemary grinned and gave her an exaggerated roll of the eyes. "If I ever get a craving for kefir, I'll remember that."

"Remember not to be feisty with your grandma too."

"Yes, ma'am." She took a drink of her sweetened milk.

"I'm glad you picked up my festival dress for me. The fit is perfect." Grannie sipped her kefir and motioned for Rosemary to follow her. She led the way back to her wing. Which really wasn't her wing at all, since she used only two of the rooms: her bedroom and the adjoining sitting room. For when Daddy got on her nerves in the main house, she'd once said.

In her old-fashioned sitting room, Grannie opened the nineteenth-century armoire where she stored mementos and trinkets that had belonged to her own mother and grandmother. She reached into the special place she reserved for her festival costume, pulled out the garment bag and revealed a spring-yellow dress with short sleeves and plenty of lace. "Isn't it lovely? Every year, when I bring home my docent dress and the tourists start coming back to the inns, I feel like the festival is finally here."

"It's the prettiest one you've had yet. Even prettier than the lavender one you sent me a picture of last year."

Then it hit Rosemary. Tourists. The festival. The inns.

That was it. That's what had been on the fringe of her mind all night. They hadn't taken advantage of the tourism industry.

"Grannie, did you say only a few guests have arrived at the inns so far?"

She nodded. "Just a handful. They typically don't start showing up until Thursday night."

"How are the inns doing with reservations?"

"About like other years. Around fifty percent occupancy. They'll start to fill up by Friday."

That was good news. "Of all the inns, how many have their own gyms?"

Grannie frowned and sat on the edge of the cranberry-colored daybed that Daddy always said hadn't moved from the spot since before he was born. "None that I know of. Why?"

"The inns might be the answer to the gym's problems." Rosemary's mind raced with ideas. "Could you visit all the inns with me tomorrow, since you know most of the owners? I want to propose that they include a temporary gym membership as an amenity. They're more likely to say yes if you're there with me."

"I'll do the best I can to convince them."

When Rosemary climbed the stairs to her bedroom an hour later, she gave silent thanks to God for her idea. This would change everything. If even half of the owners of the larger inns agreed to her plan, Abe's gym would turn a profit before the end of the first week of the spring festival. Then Rosemary could go home to St. Simons Island, knowing her father would get the boxing classes he needed and Abe would remain financially secure. A security he needed, given his childhood.

She could also enjoy the rest of her stay, since she'd be rid of the question that seemed to invade her mind a hundred times a day: Should they stay a little longer until Abe's gym was doing better?

Rosemary returned to her bed and pulled up the covers, sure to fall asleep quickly and awaken at dawn as usual, but this time with no more misgivings about leaving.

Which might have happened, if she could have erased that perfect kiss from her mind.

Chapter Twelve

Abe never expected Armstrong Kids to be packed on opening day.

He stood at the door to the childcare room the next morning and watched Rosemary register each child and give them identification bracelets. The children all loved her from the start, if their smiles and hugs were any indication. Who could blame them? She loved kids, and they picked up on it the moment they met her. It made them love her too.

Rosemary had been right about the childcare room. It was already helping his business. But seeing her there, showing love to the kids and support to the parents and grandparents and just being her usual amazing self, didn't help him to forget that kiss. In fact, it made him think of it all the more.

He looked at the clock above her corner desk.

Only eight o'clock, and he'd already blown his midnight goal of moving on as if it hadn't happened.

She clearly didn't need him, but he headed toward her anyway, dodging a couple of kids who ran in circles on the big alphabet rug. "Need help?" he asked her between registrations.

"I'm okay for now, thanks. If you want, you could remind Mackenzie to take over for me at nine. I have another idea to run by you, and then I need to pick up Daddy for boxing class."

He hesitated. "Mackenzie? Are you sure?"

She nodded. "I wanted us to get to know each other better and to talk to her about taking over the childcare room after I'm gone, so we met for a milkshake after church on Sunday. Mackenzie loves kids. She was a teacher's helper in Sunday school in two of her former churches. We talked about her duties, and we have a copy of her background check on file, so she's good to go."

"Former churches? How many of those does she have?"

"Four of her six sets of foster parents attended church."

Six foster homes? "How long was she in the system?"

"Since she was Georgia's age."

He watched his little girl playing in the middle of a circle of kids and imagined her separated from them, living with strangers. "I admit that puts knots in my stomach."

She glanced at Georgia too. "I know."

For the first time, Abe realized the enormity of raising a child alone and doing it well. Had Rosemary ever feared she might fail? "I appreciate all you've done for our daughter. You're raising her right, Rosemary. It must be hard."

"It is, but it's worth it." She smiled as if to brush off his compliment. "Did you notice that she's giving those children a tour?"

Sure enough, now Georgia was showing the toy gym equipment to a half dozen of the kids.

"Armstrong Kids builds strength and character into our smallest athletes," she said, rocking on her heels as she recited the words in a singsong voice.

"What?" Abe couldn't believe what he was hearing. "You taught her to say that?"

She laughed, giving a little wave to the grandmas standing in the corner smiling at Georgia and telling one another how cute she was. "I also recorded her saying it. Colin's going to use it in our daily live advertising clips, which, by the way, we start at two this afternoon."

"I have my copy ready for my part, but I wish you were doing the whole thing. You're better at this than I am."

"You'll do fine. Just remember to say something about Armstrong Kids and the boxing classes every day so Colin can play Georgia's lines."

"She has a line for boxing too?"

"Remember the first day when she yelled, 'Rock Steady Boxing!' at the end? Colin's using that too."

He gave a fake groan. "Between the radio and the children's skit, our daughter has become a ham."

She laughed. "No doubt."

Later, while Abe was helping Lauren process the next wave of new gym memberships, Rosemary slipped out of the childcare room, leaving Mackenzie in charge. "Can you spare him for a minute, Lauren?"

"As long as you bring him right back. Three more cars just pulled up in the parking lot."

"Bring me back?" Abe faked a grumpy tone, sounding a little like the judge. "Why is my employee treating me like her personal property?"

"Because you are." Rosemary smiled at Lauren, who laughed and handed a form to the woman waiting at the counter.

With so many people milling around in the foyer, they'd get no privacy or quiet in his open-concept office. Instead, they met in the former Natchez Coffee Shop, using the key Rance had given Abe. Inside, Rosemary sat down and slid a sheet of paper across the table. "This is my proposal for the next phase of our business plan."

He ran his finger down the page. A list of businesses, a couple of graphs. "What are you thinking?"

"You know how Natchez calls itself the Bed and Breakfast Capital of the South? As far as Grannie knows, none of the inns have a gym. I want to visit each one and invite them to use your gym as an amenity."

"Capitalize on the tourism industry?"

"Like just about every other business in town. Natchez *is* tourism." She hesitated. "And the river."

"How would this work?"

She handed him another printout. "The inns buy digital coupons from you and offer them to their guests upon arrival."

"We'll need paper coupons for people who might not feel comfortable with the digital ones."

"Right." She made a note. "Two people staying for two nights get four coupons, and we could offer family passes too. The inns add an inexpensive amenity, and the gym starts to earn money immediately, starting Friday, when the tourists hit the town."

This was genius. "We'll plan for heavy traffic

during the month of spring festival, the week of the hot air balloon festival, the two weeks of fall festival and the Christmas season. Offer the most popular classes more often, get extra towels and put them out during tourist seasons."

"And have Mackenzie bring more of her soaps and essential oils then too. They sell out as soon as they hit the shelves. And of course, lots of people visit other times of the year too. You could also offer one to anybody who comes in but doesn't buy a membership right away."

"A free trial." He reached for the paper she slid across the table. "I had forgotten how well we work together, Rosemary."

"We always did." She smiled and pointed to the top of the page. "Grannie and I made a list of our inns and bed and breakfasts. We plan to visit each one today and tomorrow."

He checked it out. She had to be kidding. "Thirty inns?"

"We thought we'd start with the largest ones, like Monmouth, the Guest House Inn and Dunleith, as well as some of the nicer midsize inns like Devereaux Shields and your neighbor, Choctaw Hall." Rosemary glanced at her watch. "It's getting late. I need to pick up my father for boxing class."

"Think he'll come?"

She let out a deep sigh. "I hope so. I'm counting on my secret weapon to get him here."

He frowned, thinking. "Secret weapon?"

"Your daughter. The ham."

Abe laughed, not missing the fact that she'd called Georgia "your daughter" for the first time. It felt good. "If she can't get the judge here, nobody can."

To tell the truth, he'd enjoy seeing the judge come into his gym, wrapped around Abe's daughter's tiny finger.

"I already told you I'm not going to that boxing class. I have a lot of research to do for a case." In his office, Rosemary's father gave her the closest thing to a scowl that she'd seen from him in the last two years.

After seeing his smile the other night.

She glanced at Olivia, who sat at her desk and focused on her computer screen, clearly trying to stay out of the conversation. Rosemary didn't blame her. "You'll be back way before noon. If you run short on time for your research, I'm sure Olivia would be happy to help."

"Olivia isn't the issue," he said, fumbling with his black robe as he tried to hang it in his office closet. Rosemary resisted the urge to do it for him, remembering how Abe had instructed the corner people to let the boxers do all they can for themselves.

"We all know Abe is the issue." Rosemary held out her hand to Georgia, who had begun to run in circles around Daddy's polished walnut desk, and led her to the window. "Look out there and see if you can find the gazebo while I talk to Grampa."

"His name is Go the Distance Grampa," she said, making handprints on the window glass.

Her father finally got the robe on the hanger and in the closet. "That is not my name just because Abe Armstrong says it is. That's undignified foolishness."

"But the classes are helping you. Do you realize you frowned at me just now? And you smiled while you were playing with Georgia."

"I smile all the time." He raised his voice a little. "And I always frown when Abe is around."

Historically, the frowning part was true.

"Grampa, I can hear you."

Hear him?

"You always hear me," he said.

Georgia kept her back to him, still looking out the window. "I have to listen hard. But not today."

She was right. Rosemary didn't have to strain as much to hear him either.

He shuffled to his desk chair, sat down hard. "You told her to say that, Rosemary."

"You know I would never stoop to that level."

Georgia turned from the window, ran to her grandfather and climbed on his lap. "Why are you scared to go to boxing class?"

No... Rosemary braced herself for the backlash to come.

Instead, he brushed his hand over the top of Georgia's head, his gesture filled with a sudden gentleness Rosemary hadn't seen from him since she was small. "I'm not afraid. Are you?"

She nodded, her loose curls bouncing.

"What are you afraid of?" he said.

"Mama and Gramma and Grannie say you're going to get sick if you don't go boxing."

What? Where had that come from? Had she somehow heard Rosemary's conversation with her mother and grandmother after she'd tucked Georgia under the covers? "Georgia, did you get out of bed last night?"

"Uh-huh."

"Why?"

"I looked for you in your room, but you weren't there. I went downstairs." She reached up and took her grandfather's face in her little hands. "Go, Grampa. I don't want you to be sick."

Rosemary pressed her hand to her mouth, her

eyes stinging at her sweet daughter's words. She caught a glimpse of Olivia, who'd turned from her screen and now swiped her finger under her eyes. How could her father's heart not respond to this sweet child's plea?

"Get my tennis shoes from the closet," he said, his voice quiet, raspy.

Georgia jumped down and ran to retrieve them as he slid out of his suit jacket.

What just happened here? Had her father actually just done something someone else told him to do? Sure, Rosemary had told Abe that Georgia was her secret weapon, but she'd thought Daddy would agree to go simply because he'd want to spend time with his grandchild. Rosemary had never anticipated this.

Regardless, she took a moment to thank the Lord.

Several hours later, when Rosemary, Georgia and Grannie returned to the gym after a late lunch, nobody could find Abe.

"He was here fifteen minutes ago, and he always checks out with me when he leaves," Lauren said, pulling her phone from her pocket and peering at the screen. "No messages from him either."

Rosemary glanced around, setting her tote bag on the counter. Things had sure changed around here. Nobody could have gotten lost in the crowd a week ago. But today she counted fifteen people in the weight room, including Colin, who'd been leaving just as she came in. The sign-in sheet at the desk revealed another ten in the new seniors' balance class and more in the lobby, early for their two-o'clock kick-boxing class.

"We go live in fifteen minutes. If Abe isn't here in five, I'll call him." Although she and Georgia could easily do the clip without Abe.

She just didn't want to.

"Grannie, come in with us and listen."

Before her grandmother could answer, Abe bounded up from somewhere in the back of the gym. "I thought we'd borrow the coffee shop for the radio spot today, since it'll be quieter. The balance class is over in ten minutes, and we have a lot more traffic through the lobby now."

Three college-aged men pushed through the entrance and stopped at the reception desk, asking to buy memberships, their loud bantering proving Abe's point. "Great idea, but didn't Rance disconnect the phone? We can't use our cell phones because service is too spotty here."

"Yeah, but I rigged up a temporary solution. When this was still a warehouse, our foyer and office area were connected to the coffee shop by a mechanical room. The door was locked from my side only, so I got a long phone cable and ran it through. I also hauled in a table and some chairs."

"You're a genius," Rosemary said, grabbing her bag and taking Georgia's hand. As always, he had taken care of the problem. "Although we'll have to come up with something else when the coffee shop is sold."

Later, when the show was over and they hung up with Colin, Rosemary pulled her notebook from her tote bag and looked at Grannie for encouragement. Her smile gave Rosemary the courage to open it.

She prepared herself to let Abe down.

Today she'd go to about any length to avoid giving him the bad news. Especially when she thought back to the look of disappointment and shame she used to see in his beautiful brown eyes in the old days. Times like her sixteenth birthday, when he'd spent all his money on his mom's nursing textbooks for that semester. Her gift had been a bouquet of blue delphinium and pink cosmos from his mother's garden, and Rosemary still had one of each pressed in her Bible. Or their senior year, when he had to use his tux money to patch their leaky roof, and they'd picnicked at Melrose instead on prom night. She'd worn her yellow formal dress, and he had on his Sunday pants and shirt.

Something about those long-ago memories tightened her throat. He'd always cheerfully given so much and had so little. It had made her want to comfort him, to ease some of his burden. To give back to him.

As she watched him now, saw the sliver of hope in his eyes, she'd give her great-grand-mother's silver locket if she didn't have to let him down.

But she had failed, and he needed to know. So she'd tell him the same way he'd told her about the tux. To the point, nonchalantly. As if the only thing that mattered was their love—and he'd been right.

Somehow those hard days together had bonded them even more.

If only he hadn't left…

She drew a deep breath of courage and, real-izing she was slumping, straightened her back. "We talked with the owners of the six biggest inns. One said yes. The others were interested, but they have two concerns. First, and easiest to fix, is what you see when you pull up."

"The front of the building?" he said.

"Not the building itself, but the landscaping. You keep the grass cut and the weeds out of the flowers, but it needs something more."

Grannie turned in her chair and gazed out

the windows. "It's predictable and rather...tired looking."

"Not sure I understand what difference the flowers make, but if that's what they said..."

"Remember who said it—the owners of some of the grandest inns in town, complete with amazing gardens," Grannie said.

"Fixing the landscaping will be expensive. I think we should offer to do the work if JD will pay for the materials. If we can solve the bigger problem the inns' owners brought up." Rosemary leveled her gaze at Abe. "They said we need more of a pull before they could commit. The gym alone isn't enough."

"A bigger pull? Like what?"

"I asked them, but they didn't have any suggestions. Two of them even said that most tourists don't want to work out while they're on vacation."

"They might be right," Grannie said.

Georgia wandered over to the counter and fished a coin from her pocket. She stood at the register, pretending to place an order. "Juice, please."

"Are you thirsty, honey?" Abe looked at Rosemary. "I can get her a water from my office."

"No, she's just playing," Rosemary said. "She drank a bottle of juice right before we got here."

"Rosemary, look." Grannie pointed at the menu on the wall above the counter. "Rance sold nothing but coffee and a few pastries."

Yes, but why did Rance's poor business sense cause Grannie's eyes to gleam like that?

"Abe, rent this space."

At Grannie's seemingly random demand, Abe frowned and shook his head a little. "Ma'am?"

"Here's your bigger pull. Rent this shop and open it as a juice and smoothie bar."

"And serve healthy snacks and desserts with the smoothies," Rosemary said.

Abe looked around the shop as if seeing it for the first time. "Have those on one side of the shop and sell coffee and nice pastries on the other side."

He was intrigued. Rosemary could see it in the set of his jaw, the flicker of hope in his eyes. "Fresh bananas and apples they can eat out of hand while they drive to work."

Abe nodded. "We could fix some of those grab-and-go bags for breakfast and lunch."

"And offer to sell breakfast vouchers to the inns," Rosemary said, "since some of them don't serve breakfast."

"Chocolate-covered coffee beans," Abe said, naturally.

"Fancy teas and tea balls. Maybe a few of those electric warmers you set your teacup on."

"Big ole Yetis for coffee." He held up his Veteran Roasters mug and grinned. "What else, Miss Eugenia?"

She paused for a moment, as if in deep thought. "Have local artists display their work and sell it on commission. You could call it Creative Juices and Coffees."

Abe laughed. "I like it."

"Could we fit the rent and extra payroll into the budget?" Rosemary asked, practicality squeezing out the fun notion of a juice bar. "Not to mention supplies, fixtures and a food-service license."

"Rance left the fixtures for me to sell for him. They're in one of our back rooms. That would be cheaper than buying them new."

"Payroll?" Rosemary said.

"That gets dicey."

The old familiar tone had crept back into his voice—the one that always gave him away. It meant that the impossible had looked him in the eye and challenged him. It meant he knew it couldn't be done, no matter how he tried.

It meant he intended to do it anyway.

This time, Rosemary would help. She turned the page of her notebook and started a list. "Mackenzie is the right age to know both high school and college-aged kids who are looking for jobs. I can get suggestions from her and find time to hire. And I'll see about the food-service license and order supplies."

"JD Turner will be the biggest obstacle," Abe said. "He already thinks the gym is going to fail, and he's just standing by and waiting to evict me as soon as I can't pay the rent."

"The gym has definitely turned a corner profitwise, but not enough." Rosemary felt her grandmother's piercing gaze on her. She swiveled to look at her. "What?"

"You're forgetting two secret weapons," Grannie said in a tone so ominous Rosemary couldn't help grinning.

"Georgia was my secret weapon this morning, and that worked out great. But I'm not sure how she can help with this."

Grannie Eugenia pointed to the floor-to-ceiling windows at the entrance, where the little girl waved at a group of three teenage girls who strode by on the sidewalk. Through the glass, Rosemary saw them smile and wave back, heard their comments about how cute and adorable she was.

"Why is everyone in town suddenly in love with her? Think about it," Grannie said. "It's because she piped up during your radio interview, being her natural, charming self."

Yes, and if anyone knew charming, it would be Georgia's intuitive great-grandmother.

"All of Natchez now associates Georgia with Armstrong Gym. Everywhere I go, people are talking about her as if she's the new Shirley Temple. Now have Mackenzie make social media pages for this shop and put her picture on them. Get her on a few radio commercials. Nothing big or flashy. Just let people know she's part of this shop too."

"What's the second weapon?" Abe asked.

Grannie straightened in her chair, raising her chin as if she'd already made up her mind that Abe would use this next weapon—or else. "Me."

Not for the first time, Rosemary's grandmother had left her speechless.

"If I manage the shop, people will trust it. Everybody in town knows how much I like health food."

That was for sure. Rosemary thought of some of her meals and shuddered.

Grannie gave her "the look" as if she knew Rosemary's thoughts. "You don't have time to manage this shop, but I do. You'll be gone soon anyway. My fifty years of managing my antiques store on Main Street gave me the skills. Besides, I'm already here every day to work out."

She was right about that. And she had the passion...

"The biggest problem I see is that all the inns

want to see the changes before the spring festival opens Friday night with the pageant," Rosemary said. "We might get the landscaping done by then, but how could we get Creative Juices and Coffees up and running in three days?"

Abe got up and paced the shop, as if his mind was turning too fast for him to stay seated. "Everything Rance used in here is only a year old. I could pay him for them right away, and then all we have to do is move them back in."

Grannie rose and ran her finger over the counter, then she held it up and examined it. "And give the place a good cleaning first."

Rosemary couldn't help but be surprised how quickly these two were putting the ideas together. "Grannie, can you pull some strings to get us inspected on Thursday?"

"Since the spring festival is right around the corner, probably so. The city officials want all the business they can get."

"Abe, what do you think?"

He gazed at her for the longest time, as if weighing some heavy issue in his mind. But not about business.

"We're not making a move before we give it serious prayer," he finally said. Then he winked at her. "But I think the Williams girls might have just saved me again."

Chapter Thirteen

Abe could not imagine he would ever feel more like a real dad than he did at this moment.

On their way to see JD Turner at the bank, Abe and Rosemary stepped outside into the perfect late-March Natchez afternoon. Georgia walked between them, holding both of their hands. He hadn't told Rosemary this afternoon that renting the coffee shop amounted to a lot more than merely getting some inns to buy gym coupons from him.

No, more than that, it was an expansion of the business that had to support the three of them. Before the sun came up this morning, in his daily time of prayer and Bible study, he'd made up his mind to send Rosemary to college. Even if he never saw her again, and even if he had to do it anonymously, he'd make sure she had the education she needed to get the teaching job she wanted.

Because during the long night, he'd admitted to himself that he was in love with Rosemary. Again. Still.

Soon he'd tell her so, when the moment was right. Or, if he was honest, he'd do it when he'd mustered up the courage, since she hadn't exactly thrown herself at him and declared undying love for him.

Of course, that wasn't Rosemary's way.

"Daddy, can we get ice cream?"

Georgia's sweet voice broke into his thoughts and chased away his somber mood. "Sure we can, honey. Right after supper."

His little girl had quickly become the brightest spot in his day, other than her mother. And at the same time the darkest, since they'd leave in less than a week. If he thought he had a chance—any chance at all—of convincing Rosemary to stay, he'd get on his knees and beg her. Buy her a ring. Put an earnest deposit on Myrtle Bank, the 1817 Spanish Colonial cottage that had just gone on the market—the one she'd loved since they were kids.

But even Myrtle Bank wouldn't entice her to stay if she didn't love him too.

Sometimes, when she didn't seem to realize she was doing it, Rosemary let that little gleam rest in her eye again as it had before. It always gave him hope until she'd pull that shade down over her emotions again. Did she love him, or not?

If he didn't find out soon, it would be too late. Because once she went back to the island, she'd never consider living here with him again.

Lord, show me what to do. Help me to prove to her that I'm not a charity case anymore, that she won't be ashamed of me like before.

If that was even true.

By the time they arrived at the bank, he'd all but convinced himself that JD wouldn't rent the shop to him. If so, Abe couldn't do a thing to keep Rosemary from leaving, and all their plans were nothing more than a dream. What banker in his right mind would lease another property to a man who couldn't keep his business afloat in the building he already had?

Then he caught Rosemary's gaze on him, silently encouraging him in that way she had.

Abe got out of the truck. He had to stop these seesaw emotions of his, now.

Inside, when they reached JD's office, Rosemary stopped and took his hand. "Don't let JD get into your head," she said in low tones. "You're doing a great job with your gym, and he'll listen to you."

Huh. "We'll see about that."

"I think he will, especially when I tell him the good news I've been waiting to tell you."

He doubted any news would help him at this point. He took the bait anyway. "What news?"

Her quick smile nearly convinced him they had hope. "I followed up with the innkeepers. Every one of them loved our Creative Juices and Coffees idea. And they're coming for a soft opening to see what we can do."

He turned to her to see if she was joking. "Every one?"

"JD can't turn you down now."

Moments later, JD met them at his office door. "Armstrong, I hope you're not here to tell me you can't make next month's rent."

"Nope." Abe motioned for Rosemary and Georgia to step inside the office ahead of him. "You remember Rosemary Williams. And this is our daughter, Georgia."

"Yeah, I heard about that." He waved them into chairs in front of his desk and crossed the room to his seat, his Italian shoes making no sound on the plush carpet. He twisted his mouth into an oily smile as he turned his attention to Rosemary. "I hear you live on an island somewhere."

"St. Simons Island, Georgia." She looked and sounded so confident and pretty that Abe recalled the reason he'd asked her to come along.

JD had always liked her, had even wanted to date her.

Maybe Abe had a secret weapon of his own.

"My appointment is with Abe," JD said, "so I'm surprised to see you, too, Rosemary."

The weasel hadn't even looked at Georgia since they got here. But the little girl sat quietly on Rosemary's lap, not realizing she was being snubbed. Or, considering how smart she was, maybe she did, but she saw through JD's well-dressed exterior and into his heart, so his rudeness was of no concern to her.

"I'm working closely with Abe as his consultant. He's made huge changes at the gym, and we're seeing an increase in traffic, sales and profit. But we have an idea for something new…"

Thirty minutes later, they left the bank with a signed lease in Abe's hand.

"You were amazing," he said. "JD wouldn't have given me this lease if you hadn't been here."

"I don't know about that. I do know I believe in you more than you believe in yourself, and that's why I wanted to go along—to be a voice of confidence."

"That was incredible enough, but when you convinced him to buy everything we need for the landscaping, I was ready to leave the room and let you finish negotiating that deal yourself."

She laughed. "It helped that his mother, who is a garden club officer this year, has been hounding him to fix it up."

As Abe pulled up to the gym, he wished things were different, that the three of them would simply go home together, maybe to Myrtle Bank. If only they could spend their evenings together, enjoying a warm, happy home.

Instead, he let himself into the gym alone and climbed the stairs to his empty, sterile, micro-organized apartment with no toys strewed on the floor and no dolls or hair ribbons on the sofa. This place needed warmth, life.

It needed Rosemary and Georgia.

Bandit raced across the living room toward him, begging to go out. Abe grabbed the leash and picked up the pup, ready to leave behind this home that was no home at all.

As usual, Grannie had taken over the hardest work.

After her run the next morning, Rosemary collapsed on the front gallery steps and found her grandmother cramming buckets, rags and cleaning solution into her golf cart. Dressed in old denim capris, a light green "I'll raise a hallelujah" T-shirt and her gardening shoes, Grannie stopped loading her cart and came over to the gallery. "Your mama wants to talk to you before you go. But don't take too long, because we have to get that coffee shop cleaned today. I fixed breakfast, so have some of my blueberry pancakes before you come over."

"Are you going now? Why don't you wait for me to drive you?"

"It's already seven thirty in the morning."

Well, alrighty then.

"But before you go, I want to know why no other king and queen couple had their picture taken together at the pageant rehearsal," Rosemary said. "And why none of the garden club ladies knew what I was talking about when I asked who else had theirs taken."

"It was all part of the job," Grannie said, hurrying over to her golf cart. "And it wasn't a lie. Cassius photographed Ewell and Martha Rose Pinkney too. They're in from Charleston and came to see the rehearsal. And Loretta and Preston Huff."

"They're all in their nineties." It was also safe to say they hadn't posed the way Rosemary and Abe had.

Granny turned the key and put the cart in Reverse, making it beep. "Get inside before your daddy eats all the pancakes."

Fine. Rosemary stood and started up the stairs.

A moment later, she turned and ran back down the steps. "Wait! What did you mean, it was all part of the job?"

Grannie waved like a 1950s movie star and headed toward Wall Street.

Understanding hit Rosemary as Grannie drove out of sight. With the precision of a special-ops soldier, her grandmother was executing her own maneuvers. Matchmaking maneuvers.

No doubt she'd arranged for Cassius to take their picture. Had she enlisted the mean girls to encourage a kiss too? Of course, she wouldn't have if she'd realized how they would shame her about Abe leaving her.

Rosemary had to admit one thing. If Grannie had meant for the kiss to drive all rational thought from her mind a hundred times a day, she'd achieved her objective.

But the kiss wasn't the only thing on her mind constantly, keeping her up at night. Watching Abe interact with Georgia, looking like the most natural, generous father ever, filled her heart in a new way. A way that stole much of the island's allure and made her wish she didn't have to leave quite so soon…

She stopped the thought before it could take root. Still, she couldn't deny that he certainly no longer looked like a man who would up and leave his daughter. Regardless of their past.

The early-morning sky had cooled and turned to powder blue, a few white puffy clouds hovering motionless as if they intended to stay there and entice her to watch them all day. But she didn't have time to sky gaze. Not with the to-do list she'd made in the dark of night, when thoughts of the kiss drove away dreams.

As she kicked off her shoes, she set aside her musings and texted Abe about her father's doctor appointment this morning and asked him to have Mackenzie run the childcare. Then she started for Georgia's room to wake her.

Mama met her at the stairs, wearing the pretty pink knee-length shorts and sleeveless button-down shirt Rosemary had helped her into before her run. "I got Georgia up and gave her the outfit you laid out for her last night. I stayed with her while she got dressed, then I gave her breakfast and now she's playing in her room. All you need to do is fix her hair."

"If you could do all that, you must be feeling better, Mama."

"I am. Let's take our breakfasts to the back gallery. I want to talk to you." Rosemary got out a tray and loaded it with pancakes, butter, syrup and juice for them both, then she followed her mother to the gallery. Once seated, Mama asked the blessing, including prayers for wisdom and direction.

Before Rosemary could butter her pancakes, her phone rang. She glanced at the screen. Tessa Louise, her boss at Faith Island Kids. She answered the call.

"I'm going to get right down to business, Rosemary. Three of our teachers are out with stomach flu. This is a four-or five-day flu, and I'm in a bind. If your mother is well enough, could you come back early?"

Come back? "When?"

"As soon as you can get here."

Rosemary tried to focus on the details Tessa Louise was giving her—who was sick and what classes needed help. But her mind kept drifting to the fact that, as daycare manager, it was her responsibility to fill in if possible. Tessa Louise knew family came first for Rosemary, so she must be desperate for help. "Let me talk to my mother, and I'll call you back."

When she hung up, her mother took a sip of her juice, as if to buy a few moments of time before starting a conversation she didn't want to have. "That sounded like your boss."

"They need me to come back. The flu is going around."

"This might be good timing. Your aunt Anjohnette called this morning," Mama said, her gaze steady on Rosemary. She set down her glass. "There was trouble on her ship, so she's coming to Natchez early."

"What kind of trouble?"

"The ship had a fire in the engine room. A few of the crew suffered some severe burns trying to put it out, but the passengers are all safe."

"Where was the ship?"

"Memphis. The cruise line put all the passengers in a hotel that night and gave them refunds."

Okay. "When will she get here?"

"She's flying in for the pageant's opening night." Mama leaned in to squeeze Rosemary's hand. "You've done so much for us, even helping Abe with the gym. I know you did that for your father. We've loved having you and Georgia, but it's time for us to let you go so you can get back to your life."

Let her go?

Her mouth suddenly dry, she took a sip of her orange juice. Of course that was what she wanted. Her home, her job, her church were on the island. Georgia had her daycare friends...

It was time to go home. To leave her parents, Grannie. Her work at the gym.

Abe could take it from here.

This was what she'd wanted, what she'd been working for. She'd helped her parents at home and helped Abe get the gym in shape. Now she could leave, knowing Rock Steady Boxing would still be here after she was gone.

That sounded as if she was leaving permanently for her heavenly home instead of merely going back to the island.

They could return anytime they wanted to, now that her secret about Georgia was out. They could even come back in April for Mama's birthday.

Strangely, these plans were as unsatisfying as the dry pancakes growing cold on her plate.

And she knew why.

She didn't want to go.

At first she tried to convince herself she wanted to stay so Georgia would have more time with her father. But she had to be honest. She wanted to stay because this was where Abe was.

The man she loved.

"What's the matter?" Mama's voice interrupted her racing thoughts. "You look a little pale."

She felt a little pale, too, if that was possible. She'd been a fool to fall for him again. He'd shown no signs of romantic interest in her. Well, except for the kiss.

Wow, the kiss.

But he hadn't kissed her because he was in love with her again or even just because he wanted to. He'd done it only to thwart the mean girls' attempt to make her look foolish, like a woman who couldn't keep a man. He'd never asked her to stay or told her he loved her.

Not to mention her father's threat to Miss Anise if she got close to Abe again.

"I'm fine." She had to be. It was time to go back to the island.

It was time to leave Abe.

Chapter Fourteen

Abe couldn't believe how much one determined senior lady could get done in a couple of hours. So far, Miss Eugenia had pulled together a crew of six retired ladies and four guys from the local college. She'd also recruited Jase to help plant the bushes and flowers that had arrived this morning. But Abe had been the one to carry the new gardenia bush to the gym's backyard. No way did he want to look at one of those every time he walked up to the door.

Bringing in a round café table with Nick, a scrawny business administration major, Abe watched Miss Eugenia in action. It was easy to see where Rosemary got her efficiency and her love of hard work. She'd done an amazing job here in just over a week. More than a consultant, she'd put all her heart into her work here. He didn't deserve that, or her.

What would she say if he asked her to stay? She'd stood by him when he needed help at the gym, and she'd made him look good in front of JD too.

Had Abe been wrong all these years, to think she was ashamed of him? How could a guy find out? He could come right out and ask her, but he couldn't imagine doing that.

No, he'd have to move forward without knowing. After all, he hadn't known she'd say yes to his proposal four years ago either.

Sometimes a man simply had to take a chance.

Rosemary breezed into the room then, taking his breath in her wine-colored dress with little flowers on it, her hair down and curly. Georgia looked cute, too, in her little pink giraffe-print dress and matching hair bow.

"I wanted to stop by and tell you I'll be longer than I thought at the doctor's office. Daddy forgot to tell me that he has to go to the hospital for routine labs afterward. He's waiting for me in the car."

"Take your time." He set down the table and asked Nick to start with the chairs. Rosemary looked a little dressed up for the doctor's office. He wished he could think she'd done it for him.

He shook off the thought. Rosemary always looked nice, whether serving as garden club queen or cleaning floors.

"Do you want to leave Georgia here?" he asked on impulse, although he doubted this overprotective mama would say yes.

She hesitated, a crease forming between her eyes. Then she glanced down at Georgia. "She needs more than just me in her life, Abe."

His heart stopped a moment as he took in her words. It seemed he'd waited years to hear this, even though he'd known he had a daughter for only about a week. "Rosemary—"

"I'll leave her with you. I know I can trust you with her."

When his pulse resumed again, he reached for his daughter's hand. "Want to stay with me and play with Bandit today?"

"Yeah!" She started to jump around until Rosemary took her other hand and calmed her down. "Where's Bandit? In your house?"

Amused that she called his efficiency apartment a house, he squatted down to her level. "He's probably ready for a walk. Let's go get him."

"I need to talk to you as soon as I get back. Can you make a few minutes for me?"

Rosemary's serious tone and unsmiling eyes turned him to ice. What was this about? She'd just trusted him with Georgia, and now she sent some silent message of doom that he couldn't begin to decipher.

Lord, what's happening here? Why the mixed signals?

Receiving no clear answer, Abe tried to shake off the feeling that something had gone very, very wrong.

When Rosemary had left and he'd given instructions to the crew, he took his daughter to the apartment and leashed the puppy. After they walked Bandit together, Georgia holding the leash, he let her bring the dog into the coffee shop to show him to Miss Eugenia.

"Daddy's training him." Georgia dropped the leash and tried to make the dog sit.

Bandit must have sensed his freedom, because he took off for the door.

Before Abe could stop her, Georgia ran after the dog and collided with the table Nick and his skinny friend carried.

Even before Abe volunteered to take care of Georgia, Rosemary knew she was ready to trust him with her only child—the only child she'd ever have. The hard part had been admitting she needed him. At least, that she needed him to be involved with Georgia's life.

Telling him she needed him in her own life— that might never happen.

With Daddy settled in the doctor's office waiting room, Rosemary pulled out her phone to check her weather app for the seven-hundred-mile trip ahead of her today. Not good. A storm was brewing and would spread from the coast all the way up to Vicksburg this morning.

She smoothed the skirt of her floral wrap dress. Maybe she'd been foolish to dress up for Abe, since she'd have to take the time to change into comfortable clothes for driving. Had she subconsciously hoped to look good enough to make him ask her to stay?

Of course not. Abe was not that shallow. Not to mention the fact that he'd mostly been seeing her in athleisure clothes since she'd been here.

Oh, and her old clothes when they cleaned up the Armstrong Kids room.

Thinking of Armstrong Kids brought a tear to her eye. What would it have been like to stay, to do more to the childcare area, making it the best it could be? To keep working by his side, supporting him and using her skills to help the gym—and him—succeed? Now she'd never know...

An incoming call popped up on her screen, and she realized she'd been staring at the weather app for a while now.

Abe.

"Daddy, I'm stepping into the hall to take a call."

At her father's snort, she swiped the screen. "Hey, Abe."

"Rosemary."

At the tension in his voice, her gut went hollow. "What is it?"

"We're in the ER," he said, his voice deep, raspy. "Georgia's hurt."

No. She stopped, pressing her hand to her forehead. She couldn't have heard him right.

"She ran into a table, hit it hard. Your grandmother thought she needed to get checked out, so I called my mom and she said to come in." He hesitated. "It might be a concussion."

The word echoed through her mind, relentless in the change it brought to her life, to Georgia's life. How can one word alter your whole world? All she wanted to do was to go back to her normal, with her daughter healthy and well...

She took control of that thought instead of letting it run away with her. This might be just a bump on the head. For now, she had to get to her child. "I'm on my way."

Rosemary hung up and snatched her handbag from her chair. "Daddy, something happened and Georgia hit her head, so I'm going to the ER." She forced her voice to remain steady, calm, as if her little girl needed nothing more than a bandage. "I'll call Olivia and ask her to pick you up."

"I'm going along." Her father got up and shuffled to the receptionist's window, presumably to cancel his appointment.

Within minutes they found Georgia, looking tiny on the ER bed, her eyes closed. Rosemary strode across the little room and touched her daughter's face. How could this have happened, after all she'd done to keep her safe the past three years? Not that Georgia had never had a bump or bruise, but she'd certainly not had an injury like this. "Georgia, Mama's here."

Georgia opened her blue eyes and held out her arms. "My head hurts."

She looked and sounded normal—*Thank You, Jesus*—and the absence of staff in the room seemed like a good sign too. If something was seriously wrong, they wouldn't leave her, right? Rosemary sat on the edge of the bed and took her daughter in her arms while Daddy stood beside it. "What happened?"

"It was my fault."

She looked over and saw Abe sitting in a hard chair in the corner, his head in his hands. "The guys were carrying in Rance's inventory, she chased the dog, and I didn't see it coming. Before I could stop her, she ran smack into a metal café table."

Rosemary's heart ached for Abe almost as much as it bled for Georgia. Surely he realized it was just an accident. If not, it was her job to bring him to reality. "It wasn't your fault. All kids have accidents."

From the looks of his tight lips, he didn't believe her.

"Did she pass out?" Rosemary said.

"No, but she cried about her head hurting, and then she threw up. Your grandmother said to bring her in."

"Miss Anise is here, right? What does she think?"

"She's not treating her. She said it's always best to have someone else take care of a family member. The doctor doesn't think it's a concussion, but Georgia has been sleeping a lot."

Miss Anise parted the curtain and came in, taking the seat beside Georgia on the bed. "I just talked to her doctor. She doesn't believe it's a concussion, and I agree. We're going to watch Georgia for a while, and if she still seems okay, she can go home."

"Maybe we should take her to my mom's tonight so she can watch her," Abe said.

"Absolutely not," Daddy said in his long-unused judge voice, his arms crossed. "She's coming home with me."

Abe stood and faced Daddy as if he realized he was going to have a fight on his hands. "You're not making the decisions here, Judge." Abe's tone darkened along with his countenance. "My mom's a nurse practitioner, and she'll know what to watch for."

Miss Anise rose and stood between them, always the peacemaker. "The chances are slim that she'll need me during the night, Abe. If she does, I'm five minutes away."

"Away from where?" Abe crossed the room, moving closer to Rosemary, his brown eyes intense as she realized what he meant.

Her parents' house or his apartment.

"I'm her father. She's my responsibility. If she doesn't need my mom's care, then I want her and Rosemary to come to my apartment," he said as if he thought Judge Burley Williams would let him get away with it.

"What do you know about taking care of an injured child?" Daddy said. "She's coming home with us, where her mother and grandmother can watch her."

And now, stuck in the middle of this, Rosemary would have to be the one to decide.

Before she could figure out what to say or do, Miss Anise held up both hands, her difficult-patient smile on her face. "Remember, you won't need a lot of people to take care of her. We don't keep concussion patients awake anymore. We don't even wake them every hour as we used to. No one has to stay up with her, as long as her breathing and color are normal and someone is in the room."

"How long does she have to stay here?" Daddy kept a level gaze on Abe, although clearly addressing Miss Anise. "Because the minute she's ready to go, she's coming to my house."

"Mr. Williams," Abe said, omitting her father's title. Intentionally, Rosemary was sure. "You rule over Natchez with a rod of iron. But I'm telling you—there's nothing you can do to keep me from taking my daughter and Rosemary home with me."

The beautiful, fierce protectiveness in Abe's eyes wrecked Rosemary. *Lord, what do I do? What's best for Georgia?*

"My daughter won't go." Daddy shuffled over to Abe and stood his ground like a Citadel cadet. "She might have made a mistake with you four years ago, but that's not the kind of girl she is. She won't spend the night with a man who's not her husband."

"Judge Williams!" Miss Anise strode four steps to face Daddy. "The objective here is to care for a little girl. Not to air your grievances at a hospital bedside."

"Let it go, Mama," Abe said, turning to Rosemary. "There's no reason the three of us shouldn't spend the night in my apartment."

From the sudden huskiness in his voice, Rosemary knew exactly what was coming. "No, Abe—"

And then it hit her. Letting all of Natchez, including her family, think she'd conceived Georgia out of wedlock was one thing. Spending the night in his apartment, looking as if they'd picked up where they left off four years ago was another.

The town—she could handle that. They were leaving as soon as her daughter was well enough. But she couldn't bear for her parents to think she was forsaking the Lord's clear command about marriage.

Miss Anise slipped from the room, saying something about discharge papers.

Her decision made, Rosemary turned to her father. "Daddy, will you stay here with Georgia while Abe and I step outside for a few moments?"

He grunted, plopping down on the bed next to the sleeping girl.

Rosemary walked out before she could change her mind.

Chapter Fifteen

Somehow, Abe knew the rest of his life would hinge on the next few minutes.

Outside, the brightness of the morning sun gave a false sense of cheeriness as Abe tried to figure out how to salvage his relationship with Rosemary—whatever it was. Because if he had any hope of working things out with her, he had to settle one issue now.

Was she still too ashamed of him to tell people they are married?

She would either accept or reject what he had to say. Realistically, it could go either way. But they couldn't continue the way things were. Change had to come today.

"I thought you were going to reveal our—secret," she whispered as if the live oaks and crepe myrtles in the hospital lawn would hear and tell. For sure, no one else was here to eavesdrop.

"I admit your father nearly tempted me to do it. But I realize a hospital room isn't the place to reveal our marriage." He took in the line between her eyes, the one that had seemed to appear overnight. "Something's changed today. What happened to you between yesterday and this morning, when you came to Creative Juices?"

She sighed, long and low, as if she had no hope.

Where had that come from? "Tell me now."

Rosemary shook her head, nearly imperceptibly, not in refusal but defeat. "I got a call from work this morning. Three of our preschool teachers have the flu, and they're going to be off for several days. My boss wants me to come back early."

"When?"

"Tomorrow."

Wait, tomorrow? "You told them no, right?"

"I thought about it, called them back and told them yes. It was before the accident. I planned to be home by midnight tonight."

"But you said you were staying until Easter."

"That was before Aunt Anjohnette changed her plans. She'll be here tomorrow. My parents won't need me anymore, and you can handle the gym from here. There doesn't seem to be a good reason to stay. At least, there wasn't until

Georgia got hurt. That's what I was going to tell you when I got back from Daddy's doctor appointment."

How had all this happened since last night? Why did it have to be now? "Can't you wait a little while?"

"My daycare on the island needs help now. But we'll stay a couple more days, to make sure Georgia can travel that far."

Abe drew in a deep breath and let it out slowly. Could the timing possibly be worse? Just when he'd realized he was still in love with Rosemary...

He scrubbed his hands over his face. Maybe he could convince her to stay until Easter as she'd planned, and maybe then he could talk her into staying for good.

But first he had to settle the one big issue on his mind.

He cleared his throat, as if that would give him enough time to muster the courage. Then he plunged right in. "For now, let's all go back to my apartment. You and Georgia can have my room, and I'll sleep on the couch."

"No."

The firmness, the detachment in her voice were fake. The tears in her eyes and the wobble in her chin proved it.

"I know you want to," he said. "I can tell. For

once, you need to stand up to your father and do what you know is right."

He winced inside. He probably shouldn't have said "for once."

"That would cause a bigger commotion with my father than you've ever seen. And Mama would chime in, too, and we'd never hear the end of it."

"Then tell them we're married. Get some clothes and whatever you and Georgia need from your parents' house, and stay in my apartment until Georgia is better. Then move back in with them if you want to."

Prove to me that you're not ashamed of me.

"No. Not on the spur of the moment like this. I need more time."

More time? "More than four years?"

She lowered her gaze to the grass. "I can't make a decision like this with my daughter in the hospital."

"No, you're stalling. Georgia isn't admitted to the hospital. She's just in the ER. My mom said she's going to be fine." He took her hand, tempered his tone. "I want to start over with you—"

The beeping of a tinny horn right behind Abe startled him. He dropped her hand and spun toward the sound, then eased up and rolled his eyes.

Miss Eugenia stopped her golf cart, Miss Cozette at her side.

Why did they make those things run quietly enough to scare a man?

"Grannie, Mama, what are you doing here?"

"Burley called and said we needed to come right over." Miss Eugenia hopped out of the cart and pocketed the key. "Why are you out here? Is Georgia all right?"

"She's fine. They're getting ready to discharge her."

"That's a relief. But why did he call me?" Miss Cozette stayed seated in the cart, guarding her injured arm. "Your father actually sounded frantic. I've never heard him talk like that before. We imagined the worst."

"Here he comes," Rosemary's grandmother said. "Just look at his face. I wouldn't want to be you right now, Abe."

What? How did Miss Eugenia know this was about him?

He turned toward the ER entrance. Sure enough, here came the judge, his face redder than a hot pepper.

"Rosemary's not listening to me at all, so I thought you could talk some sense into her," the judge said to Rosemary's mother. "He wants to take her and Georgia to his apartment over the gym. To spend the night."

This was getting ridiculous. "Tell them, Rosemary."

"Abe, please," Rosemary—his wife—said. "Just let this go."

She knew the right thing to do. Why wouldn't she do it?

"Your father's right, Rosemary," Miss Cozette said. "It wouldn't look right for you to stay with Abe."

He took a step closer to Rosemary. "Are you going to tell them?"

She shook her head. "Not now," she whispered.

Time seemed to stop then as the realization hit him. Nope, she wasn't going to do it. Not now. Not ever.

If any shards remained of his heart, they shattered now as hope left him. Left him standing there with a woman too ashamed to claim him as her husband.

Worse, it happened just when he thought he might have a chance at a happy marriage. A family. A home.

He didn't take a last look at Rosemary. Didn't say goodbye. He just turned and left her standing there with her choice.

And, for the second time, he began the rest of his life without her.

As Rosemary watched Abe stride toward his truck, a dark cloud drifted across the sky, foretelling the storm to come. But the cloud had been only half right, because a tempest had already begun in her heart.

How could Abe walk away from her again?

"Oh, Rosemary," Grannie said, her voice sounding as forlorn as Rosemary felt. "I don't think he's coming back."

"No, Grannie. He's not coming back."

When she heard his truck start up, she turned away, not willing to stick around and catch a last glimpse of him as she had four years ago. He was gone, along with any hope of a life with him.

Why had she thought things might work out this time, when nothing had changed?

When she hadn't changed.

The thought hit her like the first lightning bolt shooting down from the quickly darkening sky. All along, she'd blamed Abe for breaking them up.

Now she turned, suddenly hoping to catch a glimpse of him, see his silhouette in the truck.

She was too late. The truck was nowhere in sight.

Seeing the empty spot where his vehicle had stood, she realized she was too late for more than just a last look at the man she loved. She'd waited too long to understand him, to realize her role in their initial breakup.

Now there was no time left to show him how much he meant to her.

Rosemary turned and took slow steps toward Georgia's hospital room, having no idea how to tell her daughter that her time with her father was nearly over.

Later, at her parents' home that evening, the storm quieted to a windless deluge, its fury abated but still making its presence known. Inside, Georgia slept on the sitting room sofa, Grannie's mother's wedding-ring quilt tucked around her. Even the aroma of buttered popcorn hadn't awakened the little girl.

If Georgia hadn't been hurt and needed her, Rosemary would have gone straight to bed and had the good cry she needed. That would have to wait. Instead, she sat on the other end of the sofa, grabbed the clicker and turned on the TV to search for a classic movie channel. Wouldn't you know, *Casablanca* popped up.

She raised the clicker to find something else, maybe *Sense and Sensibility.*

On impulse, she selected the Bogie movie instead. She hadn't seen it in four years. Maybe she'd forgotten parts of it.

Two hours later, with what looked like half a box of used Kleenexes mounded up on the sofa beside her, she wiped her eyes and turned off the TV.

She was right; she'd forgotten one major aspect of the movie. Ilsa walked away from Rick for the sake of doing what was right.

All these years, Rosemary had told herself she'd sacrificed love with Abe in order to keep him safe, because of what Daddy would have done if he'd known of their marriage. But was that true? Or had she really done it because she was afraid of her father?

She had a feeling fear was the true reason. Was this all her fault? Had she not known her own heart?

Before she could explore the thought, the doorbell rang. Since everybody else was still up and doing who knew what in other parts of the house, Rosemary stayed on the sofa with Georgia.

Within moments, Grannie brought Miss Anise into the sitting room.

What was she doing here? Other than Abe, she was the last person Rosemary would have expected to come by tonight. She sat up from her slouched position, careful not to jar Georgia and wake her.

"I'm sorry to bother you, but I thought I'd stop by and see how Georgia's doing. I'm so glad it didn't turn out to be a concussion."

Grannie pulled a Hepplewhite chair closer to the sofa, and Miss Anise took a seat.

"We are too. She's been sleeping a lot," Rosemary said. "But when she's awake, she's alert and moves around."

Her grandmother sat in the matching Hepplewhite. "And she ate roast beef hash and corn bread for supper."

Their usual Wednesday night leftover supper after Tuesday's pot roast.

Daddy came in then, Mama at his side, and instantly changed the room's dynamics from genteel to abrasive, as usual. "Your son isn't here, is he?"

"Burley, when did you start being rude to our guests?" Mama said, covering for him as always.

"Since her son destroyed our lives."

No, he'd been this way as long as Rosemary could remember.

"I wouldn't say that," Mama said, settling into her recliner.

He merely snorted and sat at his desk, his back to them, as he'd done every evening since he'd come home from college, as far as Rosemary knew.

"I'm glad to see Georgia is doing well," Miss Anise said, standing.

"Your son needs to apologize to Rosemary." Daddy got up and shuffled over to Miss Anise's side. "If he won't, I'll accept the apology from you."

"Burley," Miss Anise said, "won't you ever give up your grudge against my former husband?"

What grudge? Rosemary sat up straighter. Why would Daddy hold a grudge against Vernon Armstrong? Especially since Vernon had been dead for three years.

"My grudges are my business. I'm insulted that your son would think my daughter would consent to staying in his apartment."

"No, you're wrong." Grannie shot to her feet and planted her petite self right between her father and Miss Anise. "There's no reason these two couldn't have taken care of Georgia together at his home."

"Miss Eugenia, you've lost your senses," Daddy spouted.

"You've lost yours if you persist in keeping a husband and wife apart."

No, no, no. Rosemary covered her face with her hands.

Silence fell on the old Victorian room.

How could Grannie have betrayed her, telling her secret? Rosemary lowered her hands and shot a glance at her father. His wide eyes and open mouth, silent for once, showed he had never guessed she and Abe might be married.

Her shame grew within her as she realized they now all knew she had driven her husband away after only two weeks of marriage. She wanted to grab the needlepoint pillow from beside her and hide her face in it to cover her humiliation. Instead, she merely rubbed her stinging eyes and faced them, exposed.

"What are you talking about?" Mama said, her voice shaking as she turned her gaze from Daddy and faced Rosemary. "You and Abe... are married?"

"I don't believe it." Her father's voice rose, his Parkinson's having no effect on his pitch now. "You couldn't have hidden a marriage from me. I find out about every legal transaction of any importance in Adams County."

"That's because we didn't get married in Adams County." Rosemary spoke in such a quiet, controlled voice it surprised even her. "A justice of the peace married us in Terrebonne Parish in Louisiana."

A spark shot from her father's eyes. "Rosemary, you've made a fool of us all."

"We didn't have a choice. If we wanted to get married, it had to be this way. You never would have allowed it."

There, she'd finally said it.

But how much blame was her father's, and how much was hers?

"You should have told me you wanted to get married."

"After all your threats?"

"What threats?" he said.

"That if you caught us together again, you would come after Abe and his family." Rosemary knew she was skating on the edge of disrespect, but if she didn't speak her mind now, she might never do it. And at this point, she desperately needed to do it. "That you would ruin Miss Anise the same way you ruined Cody Lewis's family. She had just gotten out of college and was applying for a nurse practitioner job. You were going to make sure she didn't get it."

Rosemary glanced at Miss Anise, expecting to see shock or at least surprise on her face. But Abe's mother wore only deep pain.

Oh... Maybe Rosemary shouldn't have brought that up in front of her...

But she had to say the rest. "Do you even remember Cody, my eighth-grade boyfriend you didn't like? You arranged for his father's job transfer to Memphis, just because you thought his family unworthy of me."

"That was different," her father said, his voice still strong.

"It was the same. You didn't like Cody because his father was a production-line worker in a factory. You didn't like Abe because his dad had up and deserted them. But instead of helping Cody and Abe, you ruined them. Or at least tried to."

She got up, paced to the other side of the room, where her father still stood. "Do you know how I found out you sent Cody's family to Memphis? It was at school the next day. We had an early-morning rehearsal for the eighth-grade Christmas play, and Cody had the lead part."

She stopped, the memory still raw after all these years. "I got to rehearsal, and the teachers were trying to decide what to do. You can't put on *A Christmas Carol* without Ebenezer Scrooge. So we didn't have a play that year. After all our hard work, we canceled. Everybody knew he and I were going together, but I didn't know he'd moved."

Rosemary turned to Miss Anise. "After the wedding, Abe begged me to leave my parents' house and move in with him at the little apartment he had on Pearl Street. I kept stalling for time because I was afraid of what my father would do to your family."

"He's not the kind of man you need," her father said. "You need someone with means, with substance. Not some soldier-turned-gym-rat."

"You're saying he's not good enough for you," Rosemary whispered.

"No. He's not good enough for you."

Wow, he'd finally said it. After all these years.

"One thing's for sure, I'm never going back to that man's boxing class," Daddy said. "And he'll never be welcome in this home." He turned and shambled toward his bedroom, where he all but slammed the door.

"Rosemary, I'm sorry it happened this way, embarrassing you." Miss Anise reached out and took her hand. From the way she looked at Rosemary, her eyes soft, she must not have been as horrified as Daddy was about the marriage. "Does Abe know about your father's threats?"

"Are you kidding? Look what a ruckus my father made tonight. Abe would have confronted him about it, and we would have had an even bigger mess than this." She had to turn from Abe's mom's gentle face. "And to be honest, I was ashamed to tell him. Abe's a good man. I didn't want him to know what my father was capable of."

"Abe knows what it's like to have a…less-than-perfect father," she said without a trace of malice. "You might want to tell him about the threats. It would make a difference."

Tell Abe? "You have no idea how much that thought terrifies me."

Miss Anise gave her a hug. "I'm glad the truth is finally out. I'm happy to welcome you to our family."

Rosemary muttered a word of thanks, not revealing the fact that the marriage was now over for good. That story was Abe's to tell. If he chose to tell it.

Besides, she didn't want to relive the moment this afternoon when Abe Armstrong walked away with what was left of her heart.

Hours later, her heart too heavy to allow sleep, Rosemary gathered her blanket and her Bible and headed for the back gallery. Earlier in the evening, she'd found her mother's copy of Pastor David's book, *The Power of the Resurrection*, and brought it with her. She'd caught Abe reading his copy in his office yesterday. Maybe it would help Rosemary too.

She settled into a big wooden rocker, the gallery's green louvered shutters closed against the rain, and turned on the table lamp beside her. Finding a bookmark she'd made and given her mother during Vacation Bible School years ago, she opened to that page.

Do you believe Jesus is the resurrection and the life? He can raise up everything that dies, not just old or sick bodies. What

have you given up for dead and buried?
A dream? Success? A relationship? Jesus
can resurrect them as surely as He raised
Lazarus from the dead.

Lazarus again? Sure, being raised from the dead was a big deal, but why was she hearing about him all the time these days?

Because she needed to hear it? To listen?

I'm listening, Jesus.

He must have heard, because she felt the sweet peace of His presence that always let her know He was here.

Grannie's door opened and she stepped out onto the gallery on her wing of the house. "Is that you, Rosemary?"

"It's me, Grannie."

Dressed in her heavy robe and slippers, her grandmother walked down the stairs and sat in the rocker next to Rosemary. "I saw your light," she said.

Rosemary handed her the book. "I was reading this. It's about Lazarus."

Grannie read the passage, then she set the book on the table. "It's about resurrection, Rosemary. Remember, if Lazarus had been dead four years, Jesus still could have raised him from the dead."

They sat silently together for a few minutes

before Grannie climbed the stairs to her room, leaving Rosemary alone with her Lord.

"God, I thought my marriage was dead four years ago," she whispered. "Now it's dead twice over. I've always believed You could resurrect the dead. Would You do that for me, for Abe?"

Rosemary wasn't sure how she knew, but somehow she felt confident the Lord would help.

Resurrection. Exactly what she'd needed all along.

Chapter Sixteen

At six the next morning, as Abe changed clothes before heading back down to work in the Creative Juices shop, he wondered how long a man could live without sleep. Ever since Rosemary came back to town, he hadn't managed more than four hours a night. Last night, none. Maybe sleep was overrated.

Yesterday's storm had downgraded to heavy rain, and Abe was thankful that Jase and the guys had gotten the landscaping in before it hit. The front of the gym looked amazing now.

But Creative Juices? Not so much. He'd done all he could yesterday afternoon and last night until the early hours of the morning, but something wasn't right. The tables seemed cramped, and the artwork Miss Eugenia had procured stood propped against the walls, waiting for someone who knew how to arrange paintings.

At about three this morning, he'd realized it was missing a woman's touch.

He refused to go there this morning.

If his mom didn't have to work today, he'd ask her to come over and help him figure out what he'd done wrong. Mackenzie had been zero help, and Lauren had the day off. The fact that he'd lost Rosemary and didn't know when or how he'd see Georgia again didn't exactly help him to figure out his problem either.

Maybe he should call Miss Eugenia. She might still be speaking to him. Or she might hang up. One thing was sure—she'd answer her phone if she wanted anything to do with him. That woman got up at five every morning except Sundays.

The person he needed, though, was Rosemary.

She'd know how to organize the delivery of coffee, fruit, dairy products and whatever else she'd ordered. And she'd know how to give the inns' owners an experience they'd never forget.

The only coffee Abe could make was the kind you get after you cram a pod into a machine.

At this point, all Abe knew was that he somehow had to be ready for the soft opening in five hours. He also had to figure out how to make the special drinks and coffees.

He was so in over his head.

Finally, he whipped his phone out of his pocket and prepared himself to grovel. He hit Miss Eugenia's number.

"Abe Armstrong, why are you calling me at this hour?"

If he didn't feel completely run over, he would have laughed at her tone. "I'm in trouble."

"What is it?"

As he'd expected, Miss Eugenia perked up at the news that someone needed her. He explained his dilemma.

"I'd come right now if it was daylight. They frown on golf carts rolling around the streets in the dark. And you know I stopped driving a car five years ago."

No, he didn't know. "I didn't expect you to come this minute. I guess I needed moral support, and I knew you'd be up."

"If you pick me up, I'll come right away and won't leave until it's done."

Thank You, Lord. Even if his personal life was a mess, Abe knew he could count on Miss Eugenia to make sure his juice bar wouldn't flop before it opened.

Rosemary awakened to a cryptic note pinned to the pillow next to her. Her heart suddenly pounding, she grabbed the pillow, flung it onto her lap and ripped the note free of the safety pin.

It was from Grannie.

Her disappointment felt like the letdown effect after an adrenaline rush. She pitched the note to the floor. What, had she thought Abe had stolen into her bedroom last night and pinned a love note to her pillow?

Come to think of it, how had Grannie pulled that off without waking her? This was the work of an experienced sneak. No amateur could have done it. *Please, Lord, don't let this be part of Grannie's signature as a matchmaker.*

One thing was sure. Rosemary would never find out.

No doubt, Grannie still had plans for her and Abe. She'd told her she'd never missed a match yet. Now her own granddaughter would be the first. A big blotch on Grannie's nonexistent résumé.

She leaned over the edge of the bed and snatched the note from the floor. It was written on Grannie's old-fashioned hyacinth stationery in her old-fashioned script.

6:10 a.m.
Abe needs help. The juice bar isn't ready for today's soft opening. He's picking me up in five minutes. You be here by eight, and sooner if you can.
Eugenia Price Mabel Stratton

Grannie was such a Natchezite, signing her full name to an early-morning note to someone in her own home. And so cheeky, demanding that Rosemary come, too, and assuming she had nothing else to do.

Which she didn't, since she'd called her day-care center on the island yesterday while they were still in the ER and told her boss about Georgia's injury and that they needed to stay a couple of extra days to make sure she was okay.

Grannie had also assumed Rosemary would want to come over and help Abe. Truth be told, she didn't want to, her old wound of abandonment freshly ripped open and still bleeding.

But what would happen if Rosemary admitted her faults to Abe? Acted out of faith instead of fear?

However Abe would take it, she couldn't make things worse between them than they were now.

He didn't really need her for the opening. He had Grannie, and she could do twice the job in the shop that Rosemary could. But, despite her earlier plans, she no longer wanted to leave town without finishing what she'd promised to do: help the gym succeed. Even though Daddy was determined to stay far away from the gym, Rock Steady Boxing and Abe, Rosemary suddenly wanted to see this through to the end.

She stretched and got out of bed. Standing in her closet, she stared at her clothes. She didn't need to try to impress Abe with her looks, that was for sure. Dressing up yesterday hadn't made any difference.

Rosemary pulled out a blue poet's shirt, a white sleeveless V-neck with a lilac-colored ruana like Miss Anise often wore and a simple beach T-shirt. When she had them all laid out on her bed to decide, she caught a glimpse of Grannie's note, lying upside down at the foot. There was more writing on the back.

Wear your muffaletta shirt.

Muffaletta shirt?

Then she remembered she'd ordered muffaletta ingredients as a nod to nearby New Orleans. Grannie must have thought it would be fun to wear a shirt that declares how much everyone loves muffalettas while serving them to the innkeepers.

Grannie also must have thought there was still hope for their marriage. If she hadn't, she wouldn't have asked for her help today. And she certainly wouldn't have told her to wear the muffaletta shirt.

Rosemary hurried to the closet. Grannie was so smart.

The shirt in her hand, she stopped. Her grandmother had shown Georgia a picture of her and Abe, taken the night of their New Orleans date, when she'd been wearing the shirt. She'd glowed in that picture taken right after an epic kiss with Abe.

Apparently, Grannie had plans.

Rosemary had been wrong. Grannie, Natchez's resident matchmaker, wasn't just smart. She was a genius.

The way Georgia kept hounding her grandfather with questions at the breakfast table, Rosemary all but held her breath, afraid her grumpy dad would lash out at her. But no, he remained patient and answered her questions. "The big white thing hanging from the ceiling over the table is a punkah fan."

"Yes, you may play the piano tonight when you get home."

"No, I don't care for any more taco soup for supper."

But he didn't have a good answer for this one: "Would you please start loving my daddy? Because I want to have a family."

In all her years, Rosemary had never heard him stutter as he did then. She decided to let him figure out the answer on his own. And to manage the rest of the conversation.

"You have a family," he said.

"Mia has a mama and a daddy and a gramma and grampa, and they have parties and birthdays together." Her little face suddenly drooped. "I just gots my mama."

He laid his hand on her head. "You have a gramma and grampa."

Georgia rested her cheek in her palm, her elbow on the table, and let out a big sigh. "It's not the same."

Her father's blank stare returned. He pushed back his plate. "Sweetheart, sometimes grown-ups can't do that. Things happen that make us... well, they make us..."

"Talk bad about people?" Georgia asked.

"Do you think I talk bad about people?"

She took her fork and pushed her sausage around on her plate. "You talked bad about my daddy last night."

"What? I thought you were sleeping."

"I was too tired to open my eyes. But you said my daddy was bad."

"No, I said he's not good enough for your mother."

Georgia's face crumpled, a sure sign tears were on the way. "No, no, no. My daddy is good."

When she began to sob and laid her head on the table, Rosemary's temper flared in a way she hadn't felt in years. *Jesus, you'll have to help me now, or I'm going to say words I'll regret.* She rose and picked up her daughter, held her in her arms and comforted her while the little girl cried, letting her father watch what his words had done.

Finally, when Georgia began to quiet, Rosemary turned to her father, who sat silent for once. "I don't think this is how you want your only grandchild to remember you once we've left."

He pushed back his chair and stood. "No. No, it is not."

For the first time in her life, Rosemary saw contrition in his eyes.

When Abe's mother's flame-red Jeep pulled up at the gym before work instead of in the evening as usual, he knew something was up. And that it probably involved Rosemary.

Mama hopped out and quick-stepped to the gym entrance in her high-heel woven sandals as if she were going in there to do CPR.

He stuck his head out the juice-bar door. "Mama, over here."

His mother started talking before she was even inside. "Hi. You need to know something about Rosemary."

Typical Mama. Short on small talk, long on things that matter. Relationships, people. Love.

And she probably thought she was coming here to fix Abe's love life. Or his I-ain't-got-no-love life.

He had to stop listening to country singers. He was beginning to sound like one.

His mother glanced at Rosemary's grandmother, who had already moved the tables and now stood at the counter, arranging fresh flowers in little glass vases to set around the shop. "Miss Eugenia, do you mind if I speak to my son privately?"

"Let her stay, Mama. At this point, it doesn't matter who hears about Rosemary and me, because it's over."

"No, I'll go in the back and organize the shelves." She peered out the windows for a moment, then headed to the back.

When she was gone, Mama gave Abe a little frown. "I didn't like your defeated tone. You've always stayed positive, no matter what we went through. I've always counted on that from you."

And he didn't like her comment. Didn't she understand anything about rejection?

Instantly he realized how dumb that thought was. Rosemary hadn't taken off with someone else, leaving Abe with two kids to raise alone, as his father had done to Mama.

Maybe he should listen to whatever it was she wanted to say.

"Sorry. What about Rosemary?"

"I went over there last night to check on Georgia."

"How is she? I'm going to see her at lunch break, whether the judge likes it or not."

"She's fine." Mama lowered her voice to a whisper. "While I was there, Miss Eugenia dropped the bomb. That you and Rosemary are married."

Whoa, he hadn't expected that. "How did it go over?"

"About like you're thinking, but worse. Abe, there's a lot Rosemary hasn't told you about her father. She accused him of something horrible, and I believe it's true."

"What?"

She pursed her lips and looked around as if making sure nobody overheard their conversation. "You should hear it from her."

"We're not exactly on speaking terms."

"Well, you need to get that way. You have a daughter. Not to mention how clear it is to everyone, other than the judge, that you belong together."

Seriously? When Rosemary was still ashamed of him? "You don't know the whole story. She doesn't want anything to do with me." He somehow needed to learn to be okay with that.

"Just talk to her. Find out the real reason she had to make the decisions she made."

Fine. Agreeing was the only way to get his mom off his back. But that would mean he'd have to follow through. "I'll talk to her."

"Good. I've always counted on you to do the right thing."

Mom was no more than out the door when Rosemary's car pulled into the juice-bar parking area. He watched her get out of the car, help Georgia out and hug his mother.

No matter how big and solid he'd built the wall around his heart, it threatened to crumble when he watched Rosemary lift Georgia in her arms and carry her to the shop. He swallowed back the lump growing in his throat and the stinging in his eyes.

It was a good thing she was leaving soon. If he had to see the two of them every day, it would kill him.

Regardless, he strode to the door and held it for them. He wouldn't have much input into Georgia's life from now on, but he wanted her to see how a gentleman treats a lady. That way, maybe she wouldn't make her mother's mistake and fall in love with some knothead.

Miss Eugenia bounded in from the back, carrying her purse, her knee-length yellow striped dress dotted with what looked like flour. "Georgia, I have a present for you in my handbag. Can she come with me, Rosemary?"

"I guess so. Then you can take her to the childcare room. Mackenzie said she'd take care of her while we serve the innkeepers."

"Good. We'll be out on the playground until then." She took Georgia's hand and headed outside.

Rosemary followed them with her eyes, then when they were gone, she turned slowly around the room. She seemed hesitant to look at him, and he understood why. But what else could he have done yesterday, when she'd confirmed all his fears?

"Abe, this is amazing," she finally said, taking it all in.

"Your grandma did it. I was ready to close the shop up again last night."

"Who put up the paintings? They look just right."

"She told me where to put them, and I drove the nails."

Rosemary set her oversize bag on the nearest table, turned to face him, and then he saw it.

I'm just a muffaletta; everybody loves me.

Her New Orleans shirt.

Memories raced through his mind at lightning speed. Jackson Square, where he bought the shirt for her. Central Grocery, where they had their only real date, if you don't count secret picnics. Which weren't so bad, come to think of it. A moonlight kiss in the French Quarter.

The bayou boat ride, when he realized he loved her.

Maybe they should go back to New Orleans...

He stopped himself short. Where had that thought come from? How did she always manage to break down his walls, even though he didn't want her to and she wasn't trying?

Was his mother right? Did they belong together?

"I called all the innkeepers to confirm their reservations. Everyone's coming, and everyone's excited." All business now, just as she'd been the first day she started helping him, she pulled her lighthouse notebook from her bag and opened it to today's page. "Did the supplies arrive? Fruit, yogurt, cream, stuff like that?"

"All here, all organized by your grandma."

"I had another idea," she said, marking off *supplies* on her list. "You could get a pod coffee maker, have a small assortment of flavored pods, and let people come in and make their own for, say, seventy-five cents. That way, if someone's in a hurry or running errands over their lunch break, they can stop in for a quick cup that won't set them back much."

He nodded, liking the idea. "I can keep some single-serving creamers in the countertop cooler and let them add their own. Have stirrers and sugar and sweetener packets there too."

"You could even do it on the honor system, with a bowl of coins and a few ones so they can make their own change."

And just like that, there they went again, riffing off each other and coming up with a great plan. Just as they always had.

"Rosemary," he said, his throat thick once more, "thank you. I never could have done this without you. Not just the shop, but the gym too."

Her smile all but stopped his heart. "I'm glad I could help."

If he let himself listen, he might hear another chunk fall from his wall.

Chapter Seventeen

In a town like Natchez, with its dozens of giant mansions, you had to go big or go broke. So Rosemary had taken a chance and ordered fresh seafood to go with her muffalettas for their opening, hoping the result would justify the cost. That way, they could give the innkeepers a sample of what they'd serve as soon as the necessary permits came through.

Maybe she'd have to take a chance on more than mere food before this day was over.

The way Abe left yesterday, part of her had dreaded seeing him today. Now he seemed resigned, sadly accepting the fact that they were through. She hadn't expected that, although she wasn't sure how she thought he'd be. Sullen? Harsh? Sitting in a puddle of tears?

Of course not. He'd never acted in any of those ways. He'd always been kind, generous, self-sacrificing. That hadn't changed today, even though he seemed more serious than usual.

As she carried plastic-wrapped muffalettas to the first table of innkeepers, she thought of Grannie's words about Jesus resurrecting Lazarus. When he died, he surely thought he was through too.

But Jesus had the last word about Lazarus. Since Rosemary had turned over her dead marriage to Him, He would have the last word about it, as well.

Now Rosemary had to survive until that last word came. Seeing Abe this morning, with dark circles under his eyes that probably meant he'd gotten even less sleep than she had, she'd wanted only to take him in her arms and soothe his heart. Just the thought of seeing him in such pain made her chest ache.

Lord, please say that last word quickly. This is killing us.

Until then, she'd do all she could to help Abe get these contracts. She hurried to the refrigerator in the back and brought out the spinach-quinoa salads. When she'd delivered them to the tables, she saw he and Grannie had been right. Including both healthy and fun foods was the perfect mix for the Natchez crowd.

"Abe, you're a born entrepreneur." Ron, the owner of Deveraux Shields Bed and Breakfast, finished his New Orleans–style barbecue shrimp and dabbed his lips with his napkin. "Everything you touch turns to gold these days."

"Nope." He gestured to Rosemary and Miss Eugenia behind the counter. "My team made this happen."

As always, Abe deflected the praise away from himself. This time he was wrong. Abe was still the passion behind Creative Juices, the gym and Rock Steady Boxing.

But for now, seeing her opportunity, she approached Ron with a pen and a contract attached to a clipboard. "Do you like it well enough to sign?"

The room fell silent as the other fourteen innkeepers all but leaned forward in their chairs to see what he would do.

After a moment of hesitation, during which Rosemary's heart came to a complete stop, he reached for the clipboard, signed the contract and handed it back. "I'm proud to send my guests to Creative Juices and Armstrong Gym. You've done well, Abe."

When somebody started clapping and Rosemary's heart started beating again, Ron slapped Abe on the back, prompting applause from the entire room.

Ten minutes later, Rosemary's clipboard had circulated through the room with fifteen contracts signed for both gym passes and meal vouchers.

"Thank you for your business," she said, holding the clipboards high for a moment. "I didn't want to mention this until now, because Abe wanted you to make your decision based on a great product that would bring value to you and your guests, not on sentiment. But I want you to know that he built this gym on a dream to help his mentor and father figure, Pastor David Alston. The heart of Armstrong Gym is Rock Steady Boxing, where Abe helps his friends to fight back against Parkinson's."

Abe immediately stopped their applause. "Sorry, but she's wrong. The heart of Rock Steady, the gym and this shop has always been Rosemary."

She slipped quickly to the back, tears burning her eyes, to escape the cheers and the pounding of fists on the tables.

Now Creative Juices and Coffees could open, and the urgency of saving the gym had passed. Aunt Anjohnette would be here today. Georgia was fine and could travel next week as Rosemary had planned. Her job still waited for her on St. Simons Island.

If Abe wanted her to leave, she could soon pack up their daughter and take off. Nothing would be left to keep her here.

Nothing except the tears her little girl would shed as she cried for her daddy.

And her own tears as she left him behind.

Her plan to keep Georgia from getting attached to Abe had failed. Just as Rosemary had suspected, he'd break her heart. But not because he'd left.

Because Rosemary would be the one to leave.

Her other plan had backfired, too—the one she'd made four years ago to keep Daddy from hurting Abe's family. It hadn't worked then, and it wasn't working now. Sure, she'd kept Abe's family safe in the beginning by keeping their marriage a secret. But had she really? When she made that decision, she'd been nineteen. She'd obeyed her father and moved to the island because she was pregnant and alone and had no one to ask for advice. At least, that was what she'd thought.

But now she was a grown woman who'd carried and birthed her child and raised and supported her alone for three years.

Then Grannie's words came back to her—the words she'd spoken the day Rosemary told her that she and Abe were married: *Lazarus could have been dead four years, and Jesus still could have raised him from the dead. He can raise your marriage too.*

Raise her marriage…

Lazarus was probably never again afraid to die after Jesus raised him from the dead. Did resurrection always kill fear? Because fear is what had kept her from being a real wife to Abe, from standing up to her father.

Then a new thought washed over her like the rising waters of the Mississippi. Maybe Daddy couldn't have harmed the Armstrongs the way he had the Lewises. It was possible that Abe, a grown man, could have taken care of himself and his family without her help. As she'd watched him do for about a decade before their marriage.

Then she realized the noise in the shop had died down, as if most of the innkeepers had left. Grannie would need help cleaning up.

Rosemary wiped her eyes and was starting out of the kitchen when Abe came in, taking a long draw from his Veteran Roasters coffee mug. He still looked exhausted, but his eyes held something else. Something new.

Something alive.

"You were amazing." His eyes soft, he looked as if he wanted to take her hand, maybe even kiss her. "Your grandma and Mackenzie offered to clean up. They're bringing Georgia to play in here while they work. You okay with that?"

"Sure, but I can help."

He leaned against the kitchen counter and

stretched out his legs. "I thought maybe we could go somewhere and talk. Someplace private."

Maybe he wanted the same thing she did— to bring their marriage back to life. "Where?" Her voice came out low, breathy.

"Rain's stopped. The gazebo?"

Oh.

She hesitated. If he wanted to end their marriage permanently in the gazebo, her favorite place would become dead to her. But if he wanted to resurrect their relationship…

"Let's go."

Minutes later, they pulled up to Bluff Park, the storm over and the air fresh, scented of recent rain and sweet southern breezes. Abe was right; they'd have privacy here. At least until the town came outside again after the rain.

They climbed the steps to the gazebo and faced the river side by side, muddy now from the heavy rains and spilling over its banks. On the other shore, Louisiana looked close and yet somehow far away, across the expanse of river.

It was a view she'd never grow tired of.

"Rosemary, I was wrong to leave." His broken tone softened her heart. "Especially on that night four years ago. I should have been more patient. I don't know why I couldn't see it then, but all I could think of was the fact that you were ashamed to let anybody know we were married. I realize you did it on a whim and regretted it afterward—"

"No!" She grabbed his arm, turning him to face her. "I never regretted marrying you. My only regret is my own foolishness."

His brows drew together as if he still didn't understand. "Why else would you refuse to live with me after we got married?"

She looked away to watch the river, its current fast, carrying all manner of driftwood as it rolled by.

Water for water. Grace for grace.

She told him of her father's threats, her fear for his family, her dismay over Cody Lewis. And he listened, silently, drawing a little nearer with each confession, each admission of fear, each apology and soft sob from her lips.

"I thought I was protecting you. And I've always been proud of you, proud of the way you became the man of the house after your father left, proud of the way you thought of yourself last if you thought of yourself at all. And now, the way you love Georgia…" Her voice cracked, her love for him and her daughter filling her heart so much that it took her breath.

Rosemary turned to him, shutting out the river, the town, her fears. "No, Abe. I was not ashamed of you."

He took both her hands and paused, his eyes looking misty and his jaw working as he swallowed back his emotion. "Rosemary, I still love you, more than ever. If you'll be my wife again, I promise to stay. I give you my word that I will never leave again."

"I want that more than anything, because I've never stopped loving you either."

"Marry me again, Rosemary? We could renew our vows right here, with Pastor David and our families. On Easter evening, as the sun sets on the water."

"Oh, yes."

Then she reached up and kissed him.

He tasted of sweet, creamy coffee and promises and happily-ever-after. But most of all, as he dropped her hands and cupped her face instead, he tasted less of the love they'd left behind and more of the stronger, deeper love of the future. She leaned into him, her fears melting away, replaced with tender assurance that, yes, he loved her. Still loved her. Loved her again.

As he pulled away, his face inches from hers, his deep brown eyes reflecting warmth and devotion, she drew in the still-lingering aromas of spicy Cajun and tangy New Orleans and the scent of his earthy cologne. Love was alive.

And she was home.

* * *

That afternoon, Abe spiffed up a little for his first meal at the Williams home and opening night at the pageant. But before heading to Rosemary's house, he had a few important things to take care of. One involved a ring and a talk with Pastor David. Another involved flowers for his two girls and a dozen roses for a certain matchmaker he was fond of. And the third—he hardly dared to believe that one…

But before he could start those tasks, he had another, long-overdue job to do. One he thought he'd have to avoid and make excuses about for the rest of his life. Until last night, Abe never thought he'd have the courage to do it.

But now he drove down the street he hadn't seen in five years, remembering the details about every run-down house and unkempt yard in his old neighborhood. Then he drove up to the ugliest, most dilapidated shack on that neglected block, pulled into the driveway and shut off his truck.

This place he'd hated, tried to make fit for his mother and brother, looked a little better than before, thanks to Jase's hard work trying to improve it over the past six months. Those were hard years, lean years, even hungry years at times. But he finally felt free of the chains those years and this house had locked around his neck.

For the first time, he could admit they'd had good times here, too, working together, laughing together. And his mom had broken free and moved forward in her dream and calling in life.

He got out, lowered the tailgate, and pulled out a shovel. With a sense of satisfaction he'd never dreamed he'd feel, Abe headed toward his mother's gardenia bush.

Later, when he tamped down the dirt around the bush's new home at Mama's Orleans Street house, the last of the tension of the past left his mind, his body.

Finally, he could go home too.

When he pulled up at Rosemary's home, she waited for him on the front gallery, looking sweet and pretty in the long pink skirt and white flowy shirt she'd worn the day she came back to Natchez. With her hair in soft curls down her back, she looked like a bride.

He got out and set Bandit on the ground, then he reached for the vases. As he started toward the old home's front door, a part of him couldn't believe he'd finally see the inside of Rosemary's childhood home. And be welcomed there, at least by Miss Cozette and Miss Eugenia. This would be an evening he'd never forget.

Georgia bounded up from the gallery floor,

leaving behind her stuffed giraffe and otter, and ran toward them. To his delight, she bypassed Bandit and flung herself at Abe. He set the vases on the sidewalk, picked her up and put her on his shoulders.

"Mama made lasagna," she said, grabbing his ears to hold on.

He climbed the gallery steps, Bandit following, and sat her down next to Rosemary. "How did your father take the news?"

"You're going to be amazed. I'm confident God is resurrecting my relationship with Daddy too." Rosemary smiled. "Come in and say hi to Aunt Anjohnette. Supper is ready."

"In a minute." He hurried to the sidewalk and came back with the flowers. He gave a vase of pink miniature roses to Georgia and red ones to Rosemary. Then he sat beside her on the wooden bench and reached into his pocket for the small box there.

"I didn't have money—or time—to buy you a ring before we got married." Abe opened the box and let her see the engagement ring. Then he slid it onto her finger. "I have a wedding ring for Sunday," he said. "If you want something different, we can exchange them."

"It's perfect." She held out her hand, admiring it and showing it to Georgia. "Not every man can choose a wedding ring his bride will love.

But you've always known just what I like—and need."

She leaned in for a kiss. This time, mindful of Georgia's little eyes, he didn't linger. But even in those few seconds, he sensed Rosemary's commitment.

"I'm proud to wear this ring," she said, her heart in her eyes.

How do you respond to confidence like that? Abe just grinned and reached into his jacket pocket. He grabbed the small envelope there and handed it to their daughter. "Honey, do you want to open your mama's surprise?"

The little girl fumbled with the envelope and finally pulled out the key inside.

Rosemary took it and turned it over, studying it.

"Check the address on the envelope," Abe said.

She looked, then squealed. "Myrtle Bank? You didn't buy it, did you?"

"I put an earnest payment on it this afternoon. But I made sure we have three days to change our minds, in case you'd rather live somewhere else."

She gave him a quick hug. Too quick. "That's my favorite house. Georgia, we're going to live with your daddy at Myrtle Bank!"

"Like Mia and her daddy?"

"Just like them," Abe said, "except better because we have you."

"I have a surprise for you as well," Rosemary said. "I called my boss at Faith Island Kids and told her we're not coming back to St. Simons Island. So you have a permanent partner at Armstrong Gym."

And that suited him just fine.

As they entered the dining room, where the rest of Rosemary's family had already seated themselves, the judge gestured to the chair to his left. "Please sit by me, Abe. I want to apologize to you in front of my whole family. It took a sweet little girl to make me see how wrong I was about you."

What? Was Abe hearing right?

"Rosemary doesn't know this, but when we were in high school, your father cut in on Cozette and me, and I almost lost her to him," the judge said in his Parkinson's-softened voice. "I've held a grudge against Vernon Armstrong all these years, and I extended that grudge to you. I'm very sorry for all the hurt I've caused you."

"And I was young and foolish and enjoyed getting attention from both of you, Burley," Miss Cozette said. "It was as much my fault as Vernon's."

"Can you forgive me?" the judge said, his gaze set on Abe.

Abe couldn't hold back a grin. "Absolutely."

The judge glanced at Georgia. "You were right, sweetheart. Your daddy is a good man."

How could Abe ask for a better end to their feud? He reached over, offering his hand to the judge, and his father-in-law clasped it, seemingly with all his strength.

Who'd have thought that would ever happen?

After Rosemary's lasagna supper, with Miss Eugenia's roses as the centerpiece and Abe sitting next to the judge, they headed for the City Auditorium. With tickets sold out as usual on opening night, the pageant was the best Abe had ever seen. Except the one in which Rosemary was queen, and he was king. But for Abe, the best part came at the end, when Mayor Russell took the mic and made an announcement.

"As you know, the aldermen created the Natchez Hometown Spirit Award this year, to be given to an outstanding member of our community and announced tonight." The mayor held a plaque high. "Our winner is an army veteran, business owner and entrepreneur. He has proven his community spirit by offering the support system and therapeutic class called Rock Steady

Boxing for people with Parkinson's, helping them to cope with their symptoms."

What? That sounded like…

He must have misunderstood. But one glance at Rosemary's huge grin and flushed face told him he had not.

"Abe Armstrong, come down and accept your award. Bring your wife and little Georgia."

Rosemary had been right. The whole town did know their secret. And as he stood to descend the steps to the performance floor, he finally understood. He was no longer a charity case.

And never would be again.

Sunday evening, Abe arrived at the gazebo early. Jase and two guys from his youth group had agreed to stand at the gazebo entrance to clear the way when it was time for their renewal of vows. Abe wanted to come an hour early anyway, since the park was now full of tourists enjoying the view he and Rosemary considered their own.

But they could share it. Especially considering how many of them they'd met at the gym and Creative Juices.

In a matter of seconds, it seemed, their families had arrived. Pastor David, Abe and Georgia took their places facing the river, and the judge escorted Rosemary up the gazebo steps.

Abe might not have heard everything Pastor David said, engrossed as he was with his beautiful wife, dressed in pink and wearing her silver locket. But he'd always remember Rosemary's words.

"I've never stopped loving you, Abe, and I'm proud to be your wife."

"And I'll stay with you forever, Rosemary."

Soon the pastor blessed the renewal of their vows, and Rosemary's kiss spoke of promise for their future. Then he picked up Georgia and kissed her soft cheek too.

"We're all married now!" their daughter cried, her sweet voice surely carrying across the river.

"An Easter wedding," Rosemary said. "Who would have guessed?"

"And from now on, we'll always celebrate two aspects of Easter—Jesus's resurrection from the dead and our marriage's resurrection."

The three of them gazed at the river for a few moments, then turned back to the narrow little park to find it filled with familiar faces. Mackenzie, Lauren and Colin from the radio station. The innkeepers, the guys from the local college, even Jase's boss, Miss Fannie. Friends from the church, the gym, their school.

Like extended family.

His heart full, he gave silent thanks to God.

Because the thing about a small town was that everybody knew your past, and they all shared your future.

Making life rich.

Nobody knew that better than Abe.

* * * * *

Dear Reader,

Thank you for visiting my beloved Natchez with me! I love returning to this charming town during the spring when azaleas and gardenias bloom in antebellum gardens.

Rock Steady Boxing also keeps this story close to my heart. My father's RSB class helped him stay mobile and encouraged as he fought back against Parkinson's. Some of the judge's experiences mirrored my dad's, including his quick recovery of the facial expressions Parkinson's had stolen. And learning to fall. I quoted myself in Rosemary's response to that escapade. I'm thankful my mom and I could be Dad's corner people.

Jesus's resurrection is the basis of our faith, giving us hope of our own resurrection from the dead. He can also raise relationships that look and feel dead, as Abe and Rosemary discovered. A relationship, dream or situation may seem dead, but Jesus can give it the breath of life.

Christina Miller

HARLEQUIN SELECTS COLLECTION

19 FREE BOOKS IN ALL!

From Robyn Carr to RaeAnne Thayne to Linda Lael Miller and Sherryl Woods we promise (actually, GUARANTEE!) each author in the Harlequin Selects collection has seen their name on the *New York Times* or *USA TODAY* bestseller lists!

YES! Please send me the **Harlequin Selects Collection**. This collection begins with 3 FREE books and 2 FREE gifts in the first shipment. Along with my 3 free books, I'll also get 4 more books from the Harlequin Selects Collection, which I may either return and owe nothing or keep for the low price of $24.14 U.S./$28.82 CAN. each plus $2.99 U.S./$7.49 CAN. for shipping and handling per shipment*.If I decide to continue, I will get 6 or 7 more books (about once a month for 7 months) but will only need to pay for 4. That means 2 or 3 books in every shipment will be FREE! If I decide to keep the entire collection, I'll have paid for only 32 books because 19 were FREE! I understand that accepting the 3 free books and gifts places me under no obligation to buy anything. I can always return a shipment and cancel at any time. My free books and gifts are mine to keep no matter what I decide.

☐ 262 HCN 5576 ☐ 462 HCN 5576

Name (please print)

Address   Apt. #

City   State/Province   Zip/Postal Code

Mail to the Harlequin Reader Service:
IN U.S.A.: P.O. Box 1341, Buffalo, NY 14240-8531
IN CANADA: P.O. Box 603, Fort Erie, Ontario L2A 5X3
